The Quorum

THE QUORUM

Joshua Cohen

TWISTED SPOON PRESS

PRAGUE • 2005

To Markéta Hofmeisterová.

And to the memory of Marguerite Stretch — The Fat Man and the Skinny Man, *and whatever the name of your story was about the little rabbit who got his new clothes dirty.*

CONTENTS

אמר רב יהודה אמר שמואל :
כל המשחרר עבדו עובר בעשה, שנאמר : לעולם בהם תעבודו.

מיתיבי :
מעשה בר׳ אליעזר שנכנס בבית הכנסת ולא מצא עשרה,
ושחרר עבדו והשלימו לעשרה.

מצוה שאני.

*Rab Judah said in the name of Samuel: Whoever emancipates his
heathen slave breaks a positive precept, since it is written, They shall
be your bondmen for ever. An objection was raised against this from the
following: "On one occasion Rabbi Eliezer came into the synagogue and
did not find the quorum of ten there, and he immediately emancipated
his slave to make up the ten"? ——Where a religious duty has to be
performed, the rule does not apply.*

Talmud — Mas. Gittin 38b

UNTITLED: A REVIEW[*]

The writing of this new history was not a writing: the slow, wintry process was surely more of an amassing. It's freezing in here — the pages are up against the radiator, and so I've turned off the heat, wouldn't want to burn myself alive. Doubtless the estimably anonymous author — no, nameless binder or compiler — didn't just go at a whim and at once to his or her local stationers, and purchase a ream and two and three and more, much more, O God much more! whole forests worth . . . and then glue or sew them all up together between two covers, without pagination, introduction, appendixes, indexes or notes or tables or anything at all. Without words, punctuation, characters. No, each piece of paper he/she and I won't rule out an *it* saved and arranged, patched together from scraps and bleached and ordered precisely — I'm speculating here — meant and means something, or not. Hard labor for a reason, slaving, or for no reason at all? and whose hard labor? Each face of each piece of paper holds something, is imprinted, scarred, somehow. Or not. And it might mean something or it might not that all of these six million (6,000,000) plus pages (an estimation, an educated guess) are blank. Pure, virgin white, like the snow around Auschwitz. Six million-plus pages might as well be greater than or equal to the palest infinity.

All of which is to write that in intent and execution this

---

[*] The following is reprinted in full from one of our more respected publications, with their express permission.

history without a title, this *Untitled* by Anonymous, is the best record of, and commentary on, the Holocaust this reviewer has yet encountered, the best in or out of print produced by, and in, the last half-century. Just as that noble laureate Elie Wiesel filled the need for a new word (*holocaust*: complete consumption by fire) for a new horror (the Holocaust), this anonymous author — if this massive thing even has an author — has found the only way to write about the event, the idea. Or not. The word is sacred, words strung together are not . . . this author didn't have the luxury of naming, of creating, of defining, merely of observing. So, what does it mean? Nothing, possibly. And what does it have to teach? Nothing, maybe . . . But it is *not* mawkish. It is not patronizing. It's not insulting. So, the skeptical reader — (and the good reader is a skeptical reader) — will think to ask, to challenge: *Well, then, what is it?*

It's an obviously enormous volume, very heavy, weighing-in at 136 kilos on my bathroom scale. In some editions, the (leather) cover is black and blank and its pages are white and blank. In other editions, this coloring scheme is reversed (white blank cover, black blank pages) . . . I know because I imagine. But it is not a diary. This is not Anne being Frank. If anything, it is an anti-diary, the opposite of selfish thoughts. The blankness actually discourages writing, the pages resist filling. Neither is it pornography. The book is free and it's sold nowhere. Mine was sent to me from the unnamed publisher, direct (the postage should've bankrupted someone), in plain wrapping without a return address (and the postmark is badly blurred) or enclosed supplementary materials. My doorbell rang, and three uniformed men, whose faces I can't recall, as huge as they were unknown to me, moved some furniture around, hauled the package into my dining room, unloaded it, put the box in my living room, refusing my questions and a tip. *So how*, that reader, *my* reader, my voice, thinks to ask . . . my voice echoes in the box, in the living room, the box where I've moved my writing table and chair, echoes something terrible . . . *how does this reviewer know that it's about the Holocaust?*

I know. I review books. These books were sent to me in the mail, in papers I reused to wrap herring and tulip bulbs. (This one was sent to me, I'm sure, unrequested.) About reviewing books, the occupation, my occupation . . . it suits me: it's a firstborn thing to do, to pronounce judgment, and I have primogeniture: I'm an only-born. My father wrote books, he wrote a book. We never slay our fathers.

I was born in Amsterdam, city of Spinoza, but some three centuries too late for him, in a century eternally late for any *ethica*, anything *ordine geometrico demonstrata*. My parents were from Poland — anglicized Kline, formerly Klein — father from Warsaw, mother from Lublin. My father truly was from Warsaw. My mother claimed Lublin, but she was born in some mudpit on the Ukrainian border she never named for me. My father, name of Józef, not *Yosef* or *Yossi*, if you knew of him (doubtful) you would have to know from his *ślepowtarza ludzie* of 1936 (*the illiterate people*, typography intentional), the first and last of his finished novels — a book I've never been able to finish for emotional, not linguistic, reasons. From a poor year in Amsterdam, we went to New Amsterdam, New York. Then we left New York, after three freezing months (the box seemingly larger than the building we were dying in, I write on a flap, then on a loose length of tape), after letters to variously placed uncles, for America. Where and when my father stopped writing books and started writing about them. Because he had nothing left to write. And I have never had anything to write at all, ever, except . . . Because what did anything mean about this: he and my mother had married in the Warsaw Ghetto and the next week were trained to Auschwitz. They survived how they survived. After Auschwitz, they robbed their way to a dead relation in Kraków, and then to Amsterdam, refusing to disembark at all through Germany.

Then I was born. My mother was fertile in that year after Auschwitz and infertile for eighteen years in America . . . here in my freezing womb. My father began his foreshortened memoirs in that year after Auschwitz and couldn't finish them for twenty-one years in America. My mother at least had me. My father had nothing. I've decided that my father's page is what I've counted out — over one full month and one sleepless night — and numbered in pencil in the upper right imaginary margin as page 3,894,764. (And I have *not* gone insane . . . this process of enumeration was the opposite of insanity, was *meditative*, ennobling . . . like prayer.) Page three-million-eight-hundred-ninety-four-thousand-seven-hundred-sixty-four is my father's page because of a printer's error there: a small, almost invisible dark dot to be found to the page's lower left, very near where the binding was. It's an impurity, an imperfection, a blemish on the fattened heifer that is this book. (Another impurity or imperfection, as impurities and imperfections are never alone: the glue is very bad, and I broke the binding of my review copy within six to eight weeks of receiving it, as I reached page no. five-million-nine-hundred-something — standing in slippers last night on the first page, tugging at the cover, to shut it, get rid of it — scattering countless pages out of order, all over my dining-room floor, pages the size of my floor. I must ask the mailman where this came from, this book which is my life, this book I don't know whether to read or not read right to left or left to right . . . and I've never even met the mailman, just leave him his season's greetings tips in an envelope. Or ask the trashman, pay him to haul it out to the curb . . . And I do not *question*: I write only now, cancelled lectures, have stopped speaking.)

And for these very defects, and for millions of other reasons, *Untitled* (better referred to in silence), requiring an entire shelf unto itself, is the incredible zenith (in the sense of *termination*) of the literature of and about the Holocaust. It reads, or doesn't read, like a Tadeusz Borowski story shorn of plot, characters and dialogue, like one of Mendelssohn's wordless songs . . . and sometimes, yes, even with this monklike vow of silence, I sing, inside the box, my cell, sing to an opening of empty wall, empty except for my father's portrait . . . echoes making me mad, but I can't stop . . . It was written somewhere, not here, not on my box's ceiling, that the one-hundredth name of God, the word in the beginning, *is* God, or at least an attribute of Him, and that this name, this word, is unknowable. Almost as if it had never existed. This book is my father's work, my father's final testament, his ethical will. This is anyone and everyone's book (drop by sometime and pick it up, please), or no one's book and it means everything, holds the light of the entire world like the facets of an infinite gemstone . . . the white pages are blinding, but I'll never burn it, no, never, must not, would consume itself and nothingness cannot be consumed . . . Its substance is Spinoza's substance, holding in sheer attributes and modes all that was and all that will be, and it means nothing. I sit on it, the book, high, high up, to eat my cold breakfast, herring, off the top of my mother's old wardrobe (refrigerator moved upstairs to my bedroom), the wardrobe the only other thing that fits in my dining room anymore . . . eating in silence except for my chewing like a cow. This review shouldn't exist, now or ever. *Untitled* in an all-parchment edition (cover and pages) is scheduled for release next spring.

Postscript, Winter: *This reviewer has just learned through the mail that* Untitled *is* Volume II *of a two volume work.*

BENJAMIN KLINE

THE TRIAL

May it please the Court:

Respected gentlemen of this heavenly jury, you have heard many things today. You have heard testimony — from parents, family, friends, acquaintances, even my client's Evil Urge . . . and I caution you against considering *His* remarks . . . You have heard the grandiloquent closing statement of my esteemed and formidable colleague, the Prosecuting Angel. My own closing statement won't be long, certainly not as sustained as that masterpiece of oratory just offered unto us, just placed high on the altar of your esteemed judgment, a sacrifice of much learning and thought. Still, it's not enough, not worthy of you, of your purpose . . . The problem with all of my closing statements is that they're always and necessarily shorter than the lives, or afterlives, they are intended to defend.

I will agree, somewhat, with the Prosecution: of late argumentative about everything other than matters pertaining wholly to his occupation, yes. Admittedly, he owed the candle-maker for a month's worth, a debt which my client's daughter has now paid from the sale of his chair and desk. Possessed of a wandering temper, yes. Innocent ad aeterna of any modesty that held no possibility of his temporal enrichment, okay, fine, yes.

But my client, Reb Schrieben, better known to you, learned gentlemen of the jury, as the Nachmachen, was nonetheless a man of estimable holiness. An ascetic, surely, though one whose asceticism raged only against the temptations of the world below ours, a world I'm sure you'll all remember.

In matters of the sacred, his heart was as superabundant and unyielding as his womenfolk would allow. How he married is not of interest to us . . . suffice to say he was kind to his wife while she lived her short life, as she stated unequivocally in her emotional testimony earlier, and I quote: *He treated me as one would treat the Queen of Sheba*, end quote. That would make my client a Solomon. Yes, the existence of personal miracles does not depend on the Nachmachen's belief in them: he was once a kind and easygoing man. After the death of his wife, though, he believed only in work, or, more accurately — for his occupation necessitated a fanaticism for accuracy — he believed in service. That is his word, I remind you: "service."

You have learned that he was a Sofer, a scribe, one who wrote the scrolls of the Law. But not writing exactly. The work was more like copying, the job of an applied student. He was the taker of murmuring dictation spoken long ago in a Land he would never walk three cubits upon. Instead, he sat in Josefka — which, if you should ever have the opportunity while on a terrestrial holiday, you should never visit — and he worked. Every letter he copied, every word. Look at his hands! Hold up your hands! 72 years he sat and did this and not mistake one, not even in infirmity and encroaching old age, not a slip.

Yes, what he did was rote, an animal's work. Yes, what he did was an occupation directly opposed to the spirit of his own people, who did and made things, his people who redacted and reinvented and reinterpreted themselves every other long season, who flaunted the Second Commandment. But he did his job because somebody had to do it. And so why not him? I ask, why not a man whose talent never usurped his need? His task

— as I am sure you'll recall from your studies, however distant they are — his task is one of the most respected, even revered. His was a holy calling. You might think that he wrote, or copied, for himself only. That there was only one shul in Josefka and what did it need with hundreds of scrolls. That most of the scrolls in his hand, stayed in his hands. But, I ask you, is that not love? passion? The work is never over. How to trust your work to others with the ways down there these days?

And he was good as no one else was good — you've heard the expert testimony, my examination of the Rabbi's son — yes, he was meticulously good. If God Himself — blessed be His name forever and ever and may He forgive the following heresy — made a mistake in the original, then there was a mistake in each and every one of the 612 scrolls the Nachmachen turned out. And, gentlemen of the heavenly jury, there's a teaching to be found — I'm sure the venerable Prosecutor can tell you where exactly it isn't — that runs that God didn't make a mistake, to err is not divine. You remember: that God didn't even write the thing. He dictated and Moses took it down, the great leader an unsalaried secretary, days long on Sinai. And so if there was a mistake, it was mortal. And if there was a mistake, then it was handed down: it was repeated through the generations unto generations in nearly immortal faithfulness. This is the holiness of the Sofer, striking a rock so ink issues forth. The Nachmachen, Moses' distant successor, was also mortal. Mistakes he also made. But mistakes of what nature?

His life, then, an unfurling parchment: you will recall that in Josefka at that time, all the animals, all of them, had died. I refer you again to the testimony of the Rabbi's son — these deaths are to be attributed to the milk. And so for a period there were no more animal skins. A few feathers for quills and the organic ingredients of the proscribed ink, he had. Skins, parchment, he didn't. Again, the testimony of the Josefka Rabbi's son, sorrowfully a recent addition to our ranks, also taken by the milk. This exhaustion of resources was a disaster for the Nachmachen, financially, and, more importantly, for his soul. The people would always require the Law and the Nachmachen required his parchment. No Law, remember, with no parchment . . . you want to talk about sacrifices? As the Nachmachen testified, he initially spent some days on a new regimen, practicing particular ornaments one thousand times, evenly spaced, on his walls, never on his floors . . . Please understand, gentlemen of the jury, this man sanctified his skill. Dedicated it and rededicated it daily. No vanity here . . . or sometimes — we all can understand, I'm sure — humility and vanity become confused.

And so, with no resources with which to produce, or reproduce, the Law . . . and which is the true Law, the Sinai-original or some latter version? . . . with no parchment then, yes, the Nachmachen started on skin, human skin, not his own, the skin of Surly, short for Israel, the husband of his loving daughter, his son-in-law. He never dared attempt her skin, his daughter's. Let it be remembered that the thought of uncovering her nakedness fevered him. That is the one remark his Evil Urge gave in His testimony that I believe to be veracious. She, his daughter, is still among the waking, thanks be to God. She is relatively young, and so we're unable to have her testimony . . .

remember that only the dead are allowed to remember, all. Though this act of writing on skin was forbidden, the Nachmachen wrote and wrote. Such was his passion: Genesis on the right eyelid, Exodus on the left. Leviticus sloping down the nose. Deuteronomy across the upper lip as small hairs grew among the many repetitions and formulae. My client is and was aware of the prohibitions. How? Well, esteemed jury, had he not traced them maybe thousands of times? Is the sin not the repentance and the repentance not the sin? But the Law only instructs not to *gash marks for the dead*, or *to incise*. The body is God's, blessed be His name, and is to be respected is the idea. No one bled, carved chapters into skin with a stylus. The Nachmachen, with his daughter's supervision, made sure, testing on himself, that the ink was not harmful, that it would not seep in and poison his son-in-law. And Surly — who, thanks be to God, is also alive and is expecting his first son shortly — attended the mikvah once a year, between the New Year and the Day of Atonement, after each completion of the cycle, turning the water dark and thick, dripping blessings and curses in equal measure on his way to shul. (*The Law washes off?* asks the Prosecutor, *a washable Law?* and I say *ritual purity* of the highest order.) Three cycles were completed in this way. Three! Surly and his wife, my client's daughter, went away when Surly took up a job as a shoemaker in the capital city.

So, in an empty home, the Nachmachen sat, mourning his life already, at his table. Such emotions when he was prevented from putting down the Law! My client set out to write onto parchment of ink. Yes, he wrote with ink on parchment he made, dripped, out of ink. Ink on ink. The Law blurred on the

Law. He would ink the air in, and write on top. Since all words are contained in all the letters and all the letters contained in all the ink, he wrote conceivably infinite scrolls worth. Sometime later, he began writing straight onto nothing, ink shaped finely in air, air-shaped ink. He let the drops drip into space. Remarkably simple, yes? Like writing on regular parchment, except without the parchment. The Prosecutor insists, perhaps he believes benevolently, that my client had by this juncture lost his mind. That he had gone insane. But I'm not seeking that loophole. That's not who my client is. We won't bow to that offer. Remember: the easy path leads to the world under the world we are above.

At first my client wrote individual letters, for practice, then words and then whole sentences, then chapters, books. Into air. The letters were floating there, readable the right way from both sides, as, as we are taught, they were at Sinai. My client was not aping God. No, he was praising Him.

And then, his unspeakable end, which must be spoken . . . the Law written, must be read, in public, I remind. Yes, admittedly, he once forgot it was Sabbath, and may you and the Lord of Hosts forgive him, and he wrote through into dawn and further into night. But he had no womenfolk to remind him of the hour or the day. And most of the residents of Josefka had by now abandoned him, the sinners they are . . . I await their trials in this courtroom with sympathy and yet eagerly, someday soon I believe. And yes, he wrote the Sabbath longer and night got blacker and blacker, like ink it was raining from the heavens through the holes that are known as stars. We are prepared to admit it: frenzied, my client stopped copying . . . but that's how it's been presented to you. This is the beginning of what my esteemed friend the Prosecuting Angel seems to regard as my client's most terrible sin. Or mistake? A sin, I submit, is a wrong thing done well. The Nachmachen unwittingly moved straight from copying to original material, within one word, in the middle of the most-used name of God, yes. This is inspiration! New stories, new endings, twists and turns, many of which were presented as evidence today. Who could forget his eleventh commandment?

Thou shalt not stick thy nose in the, pardon, tush of thy God.

Who has not heard breathless — though we no longer breathe — his story of Moses which omits any mention of Moses? How did you find them, Reb Schrieben? Incredible. The letters were his letters now — the Prosecutor has stated outright — the words his words. Wrong. I insist that soon they weren't letters or words at all . . . they were inspired! prophecies . . . a new world . . . shapes inked, to fill out the void. And we all know the void, don't we? How lonely it is. All the writing on the last wall, as that Biblical story goes, and yet, who can read it? The Nachmachen set out to remake the world as Law, the highest sanctification.

And then, yes, then came the little men, crowns with crow's feet. He inked them into animation, we admit. They walked, though, I might remind you, they didn't talk . . . at least they couldn't testify today. He inked them into perfunctory tasks: a golem staff of inked attendants doing the laundry, preparing hot meals, light housekeeping. He did all this, I insist, to keep his mind focused solely on creation. And creation to honor God Almighty. So great was my client's skill that the inks would run together, forming a larger man for a larger task. Then the strokes would seep out and scatter into the neglected pantries of his household. Always he and he alone swept them up and buried them in the ground as the Law instructs, tiny graves. My client inked into space signs, needs, desires, worlds entire. Yes, this was prophecy! All to glorify Him! The inks frolicked, dripped like wet and ripened fruit, and multiplied, and soon there was no room around the house, no room around the Nachmachen, no outside world. He had, and he admitted this to us all in open court . . . he had . . . his words were, and I quote: *I had overstepped*. Such modesty! Even in his modesty is he modest! As he recounted here today, everything was heavy, full of ink, one enormous ornament. A mistake or not, learned gentlemen of the jury, I hold there's no difference here. And there was no more space for him. The creator had no more space in his creation for himself!

So, knowing his sin, he repented. One of the purest acts I have encountered in my innumerable years in this position. He inked himself into the doorway of his house. And then inked himself in, filled himself up, swallowing whole wells of the stuff: inked in his heart, liver and kidneys, ink in the lungs, ink in the ears, nose and throat. Ink in his veins. Gradually everything faded for my client. He had written the Law into himself. Not on his arms and on his head as reminders, but everywhere, inside. He drew in his sin. This is how much he yearned for the absolution of the Law! The Prosecutor has alleged, has done everything short of outright accusing my client of suicide. But it was not suicide, no . . . But if the only repentance fit for the sin was suicide? is suicide forbidden in this instance? Anyway, feeling heavy, he fell. By falling, we rise, I only remind, we sin to merit.

He was buried poorly and his daughter was never even notified. Yes, the treyfheaded citizens of Josefka will get theirs . . . Yes then he rose, to sit on trial, before you, today.

Esteemed and learned gentlemen of the jury, I urge you to be careful in your deliberations. Let my client stand as an example: as much as my client demanded and exacted from himself, demand and exact the same from yourselves.

Weigh him on the scales most high — placing my task in this hand and your task in my other, your purpose, my head as the indicator, I shake *no, no, no* . . . one of my hands, your hand, the outstretched hand of judgment, I place on this floor which is my client's heaven. I ask you to appreciate your divine responsibility. I thank you for hearing me out. I have been the Angel for the Defense for long enough. My mouth has done its share before.

Gentlemen, this is my job, I handle all — you should have my caseload! — number the line of holy people at my door, knocking, day and night, night and day, all with their appeals, their grievances, all with their demands, wailing the promises they seek fulfilled . . . But the Nachmachen's innocence is the purest innocence I have ever encountered. Admit him to Heaven without delay, and if you do, the first thing I'm sure he'll ask of the Angel What's His Name is a chair, a desk and his tools. No hogging the celestial banquet. No loafing. This was not a life lived for the sole purpose of achieving salvation.

My client had other responsibilities. He had, perhaps, too much passion — but passion, respected gentlemen of the jury, like all the inexplicables, is God's, and only God's, to give.

A REDEMPTION

But the eruption of a work of art presupposes that the author has come into being, you wrote, Herr Doktor Franz Rosenzweig, *The Star of Redemption*, Part Two, Book One — I copied it down, white notepad, under the sink. But would you still agree, man with the wrap around your neck in the photograph? This is something, then . . . and who hasn't not read Plato's *Ion* these days? Your photograph, Rosenzweig, dated 1929 — a lifetime before my birth! — I've taped over my bed (but not the bed I was born in), scissored from an outdated edition of an encyclopedia of your people when Samuel wasn't watching. I put your picture up because I wanted another failure in the room. Failure, because this is how I understand it: you wanted to convert to Christianity and you announced this intention to family and friends, but before you plunged you decided to endure one last Day of Atonement. (As if you didn't observe the day, the day wouldn't exist!) Upon leaving the synagogue that night, after the Book of Life closed, you had decided that you would remain a Jew. And even more: you decided to devote your entire life to the renewal of your people and its religion — do I have my facts? And then you write your masterpiece, a portion of which I've quoted above, the whole thing a load of theosophical mystification with a few pearls cast in here and there. Your aim was to have Christianity (and Christians) accept the historicity of their religion, to have them view the modern world, whatever that means, as the apple-shaped earth of revelation and not the earth-shaped apple of original sin. And as for your Jews:

you wanted them to live inside and out of the world simultaneously, like worms on the fruit, surfacing and then again burrowing into the core . . . your ideas: green snakes with apples for heads, no senses except their tails, slithering over and around, colliding, crashing dumbly into each other forever and ever. And I am as insane as you were. I too need to pour myself out into anything that'll have me, I too need to knead the world and nothing less than the world. You have my empathy. To what ends, then, have I, reckless as you, applied myself? All my work, my false work, is messily filed. I have made what I have made. And only now I will be, will I become. This work, my past prior to any past, is necessary to my future. It is the enduring foundation of my temple, the skeleton of my future presence or . . . maybe it's all the inner life . . . *Organon* mediates *Organ* and *Anon* . . . The making of something is less than half though, man whose wrap in the photograph keeps his head on. The other half, far more difficult as to frighten off the Idea itself, is naming. And so to prove my worth to the past, I'll give myself a name, give myself a life, please, moment. Maybe Ari Stern. Remember it. Inscribe it upon your hearts and on your doorposts and heads and arms and remember it when you rise up and when you lie down and on and on and everything else. Ari Stern, a familiar name, easy enough, though I'm . . . Ari meaning *lion* in Hebrew. This doubtless amounts to nothing psychological or real. Other names, mere possibles, nothing blown deliberately: Jacob Stern. Even Franz Rosenzweig. Agnes Stern née Sterbe . . . (yes, now Agnes Sterbestern). I should . . . maybe I should have been a woman. I will be beyond sex, or of a sex in the middle (the sex of legend), not here, not there, legend. Everything in your life, reborn man with the wrapped-on neck in the photograph, sick man, 1929, everything has presupposed me, my works predate me, and I do not exist yet. I will idle my true existence, my work already done, away. This note is my last . . . I have a reflection in the half-opened window — let us name him too. He left university at the start of the semester of graduation and I don't know why . . . went to work in the university's library among his former peers, eight hours, five days per week, as their servant, a servant also, incredibly, to Samuel. I found things, looked things up, and that's how I found you, Rosenzweig. Willingly austere period in his life, he'd moved out of the house and into a peculiar sort of terrestrial hell known as a *studio apartment*. Then he had three passions — passions are had in threes: music made with the nose (nose-harp, nose-flute, inhalation, sneezing), the philosophy of Hegel, and aphorisms. He made a list of these, aphorisms, a small notepad full — you'll find it dripped-upon, under the sink — and read them to a redhead at a local pastry shop where he drank also when he had money. The aphorism phase was when he realized that none of his thoughts were at all focused. When he was sober everything was a half-truth and when he was drunk everything was three times that, truth. It never erupts, truth, and nothing else does either, not in my experience, nothing except ambition. Out of the book and *Ins Leben*? I am quite the opposite, Herr Doktor — and what's the difference anyway, between books and life? But you thought Ari Stern, meaning me, will be an author, an artist, a maker, and I will not, will not or never be . . . I will be an idea, beyond discipline. I have began much and ended nothing, except this . . . I have thought much and written maybe only a third of it down. I have thought much and put so little into action, plans . . . *ideas*. I have redesigns for the subway system among other things (concentric circles), an idea for a large municipally-funded park where people of all religions would be paid to pray as living sculptures. I am a movement, understand, just not yet. When you, not you, find and read my papers. My parents, your religion, your religion and my parents', condemn what I will do, have done . . . But a man who does not exist — and by Law and by law I am a man — that man, that nonexistent man, does not have parents. And if he does not have parents, he does not have religion. When I exist finally, when I have redeemed myself, I will invent my own religion. Read on, blue notepad, last ten or so pages. There I retell the story of Moses omitting any mention of Moses. The religion that I will invent, and shirk subsequently, will be a religion that worships one god, though my one god will not be the one god most people share. That god will be me, understand? An idea is as a god — *idea*, a scrambling of *A dei* (and obviously a mediation of my *I* and a *dea*, which has other implications, embarrassing, red-headed . . .) — and I will exist as an idea only. Rosenzweig, I want to *do* something, want to empty myself into history and who am I? You were a Jew, Rosenzweig, and you at one point wanted to become a Christian, but you stayed a Jew, a living death, slow. But you should have become a Christian — baptism isn't the only way to redemption . . . there are more permanent salvations. Even now, though, my likeness exists — has she shown everyone the album? But the photographs are false. I'd never allow myself facial hair, I'd never wear that ripped jacket. He will have ego (taking dictation quickly, proving unable to avoid Freud's obscene *Ich*), such force of mind, the work that I've done and such wandering desire will make that so. And such are the things, the wandering force and the work, that perpetuate my present anonymity. The window is now fully open and the air is dark and warm. None of it, understand, is juvenilia, or, more accurately, since life is juvenilia, then all of it is juvenilia. But all the things are very real. They, the piles, are under the dresser too, everywhere. Only after this, after doing this, will I exist, will I deserve to. But who am I to know of him now, so early a voice of acclaim? I am no one. I have given him . . . him, this inaccessible dream, my influence, my fame . . . I've given him my name to somehow perpetuate my memory after I am gone, soon enough. I was born premature and I am premature and that is how I will die. My father Jacob, a lawyer who knows what there is to know about legacies from the practical angle, and my mother Agnes, a wife of a lawyer and already an adept in the rites of mourning, will survive me fine, the wound prior to the fall and all. Stars are dim from here, sitting on the windowsill, nothing up there pointed, only dulled, and he should ascend. You will all know me as they make me, remake me, after this, when I leap for the stars from the sixth floor — that is the only way you will know me. *All cognition of the All originates in death, in the fear of death*, you write, that's your first line, and I would agree except for the last clause, which, now agree with me, was conceived in fear. I have no fear or at least now I don't remember fear anymore. Nothing is accomplished late and there is no early anymore, yet. The eruption of an author, a maker, presupposes that his art, his work, has come into being. I wrote down the aphorisms because my memory is as weak

♦
♦

My son my only and firstborn son Ari wrote the above and leapt and fell and hit and we buried him yesterday and I found this in the dump where he lived — I didn't know where he lived until two days ago and now I know and moving out his stuff today, the day after, two days after, I find this and some other things, six boxes full actually — and I will give them after shiva, all of them, to his uncle, my wife's brother, who is the head librarian at the university who gave Ari a job when he insisted on leaving and now he's left everything and I hope Sam, please Samuel . . . my dear brother-in-law, you were his uncle . . . I hope he will find some merit here, some worth, I do not.

LETTER ABOUT HAIR

Dear family and friends at home, from me, on the other side,

Six marriages worth of apologies for not responding to your three letters, Mother and Father, postmarked I can't tell and received who remembers. Your son, understand, has been busy, occupied . . . but I don't need to tell *you* about occupation. Six marriages worth of excuses too, though all of them legitimate. Life is fast, fleeting in this Promised Land . . . which words and idea have always interested me, their not indicating Good or Evil, only promise and its fulfillment. But what exactly *is* the promise? And is it worth depending on? Is it the type of promise that's best left unfulfilled, like the one of the Messiah? Questions are the promises of answers, and I endeavor to fulfill, if not in this letter then in ones to follow, to answer the questions you've put to me, as best as I am able.

Due to the volume of letters I've received from those I've left behind (R., T., Fat A. usw.), I ask that this note, or its contents conveyed in another form, be posted for all to read in the Town Square, thus saving me much repetition and precious time. Or put it on file in the Town Hall, or read it aloud the way Mother said they used to do before what happened — and nobody here *knows* what happened, and so they're able to live their lives relatively effortlessly. They don't have all the distractions of history and Halls and Squares. Here what we — I do not know why I write *we* — what we lack in Town Halls and Town Squares, what we lack in history, we make up for in *opportunity*, possibility. No one will read this letter from the time I seal it in an envelope to the time it leaves these shores. I wouldn't be amazed if I could set up my own Town Hall here, and if I did, they — whomever they turned out to be, not that I'd have any choice — they would come. Actually, the drinking establishment in which I write this is named the Town Hall, and it's proved a very suitable establishment for my purposes . . . I'd love to one day share with you.

You ask about money — obviously a serious concern for those of you considering immigration. The ingenious citizens of this strange apple have devised a progressive economy, a Revolution that puts ours to shame. And this will be the subject of my present statement.

Yes, certainly bring your underclothes, some vodka wouldn't hurt — the vodka at the Town Hall is lacking — but, most importantly, bring hair. This country's currency is hair, human hair. Human hair is redeemable for any and every imaginable good and service. And so shave yourselves! Shave you mother! Shave your brother! Shave your children too! Though some people cheat by passing off dog and horsehair as human — you might be tempted to try this — but the penalty is death . . . but, then again, death here is arguably preferable to life there. And that's how some things cannot be translated . . . (Is my language still good? Am I still earning my high marks, Mother? Or have I forgotten and is all this incomprehensible? Leave this part out and continue . . .) But then again, we have more dogs and horses than they do. Our horses, in a dark market, would make us millions — they, thankfully unknowing, are themselves most prosperous citizens over here — but they graze so far outside the city, I'm told, and I admit that I haven't seen one yet. And it's hard for me to see, anyway, with all this hair I've been growing, grown over my eyes now — I'm growing hair the envy of all . . . *we* all grow hair better than *they* do. I'm growing it to treat our town's next arrivals to cake and coffee, at an establishment of everyone's choice, and maybe to a spring wardrobe. Yes, spring wardrobes for all! Lightweight fabrics of one season's warranty . . . Things are so different here.

I've never sweated this much, sweated here in a month what I sweated back home in my whole life prior, and you can leave this out — yes, please do. To recap: bring bags of the stuff, hair — we have enough, don't we? We can flood their markets, bind them in our locks.

But what is the hair used for, you ask? Wigs are one thing. All the inhabitants here are bald — I suspect even their God is bald, and you can't be imprisoned here for saying or thinking that. Yes, it's the heat that burns it all off — this execrable heat and everything smells with the heat and this much hair. Yes, but in a place so hot it's an effort to grow hair, a labor, an application of all thought — Mother, don't laugh and roll those jellied eyes, your son speaks the truth, across the ocean through the horn you hold to your ear as Father reads these words — you can leave this part out if . . . you should leave this part out, if only to save yourselves the undue embarrassment when the whole town has this read to them by the Mayor Whomever from the plinth of the statue of St. Jude Thaddeus in the Town Square . . . no I haven't forgotten, and I know you're still beautiful J.

And the official letter, uncensored, may continue now:

stockpile the stuff! The idea is that your hair — some of the highest quality hair in the world according to the most respected of independent estimates, according to various high-placed and recently acquired friends of mine — that your hair can and will, if you decide to immigrate, make your life easier! No more hair to wash and manage — just shave and sell, shave and sell and shave and sell and shave!

Here are some prices which may or may not inflate by the time you arrive on these shores — so don't quote me to myself when and if you arrive, and when and if you find me by then, living in my mansion in the Hills, and I'm just joking . . . they're, the prices, just to *get an idea* as they say here:

> — *A "Ranch-Style" House in Joisey: a full head at shoulder length.*
> — *Strudel, one piece (not like they make it at home): 2 cm. / one head strand. 1 cm. / one head strand, red.*
> — *One hour with an Oriental woman (yes, they have those here, and use your imaginations): two full pubic strands, lengths negotiable.*

So what else do you need? What further enticements? Hair, *the ever renewable commodity*, they say — the stuff falls off you, even grows for awhile after you die. Yes, some unscrupulous people disturb the bones, and maybe you should too, bring them with. Is this not the foretold resurrection of our ancestors? No, Mother, I haven't forgotten my God, the God who can't be imagined . . . and if He *is* imagined . . . (forgive my blasphemy committed only to *drive home a point* as they say, as they drive drunk friends home over the river), if He *is* imagined, I would imagine He'd have numinous hair and a luminous beard covering the Throne unto the Footstool. Yes, bring our God, but forget your Samson, abandon him, him alone. They, our dead, can live with us too — their hair can at least — and their deaths will contribute substantially to the quality of our lives, our enjoyment. Yes, life can be enjoyed, that's a possibility, an *option*.

My friend here, I call him Layer Man . . . known to me and my acquaintances here as such due to his insistence upon wearing multiple layers of clothing throughout the year, and *in this heat*! Claiming that he is, exists as, layers only, that he's a substance of layers and that if he removed them, the layers, one by one, thinner and thinner — fur coat the outermost and who knows what the innermost — that he'd eventually disappear altogether, cease to exist. We were roommates for a month — anyway he says *Hello* in our language which he knows half-much because *his* language is *half* ours — and I suspect, after living with him, after sleeping in the same bed, that underneath all those layers, those peels, he's hiding a body spectacular with hair. I say this because he's here with me, and he's *paying for this water they call vodka*! And I've drunk quite a bit of it — it's supposed to promote growth.

And so it's hair here — after what we went through, could that be so surprising? . . . and are any of you still alive, or does this letter sit in an emptied office for the dogs to sniff and then eat at (I'm thinking of licking this envelope, my early breakfast or late from yesterday) — a forspeizen before they eat each other? The answer to everything, so says Layer Man, a former professor of history and a man who, for nothing, provides me with tonsorial support whatever the hour, is *probably not*. He's a former professor of history at a distinguished university, a professor over there too, quit, he says, years ago, quit after the Revolution (the one here, peaceful) because who needed to work anymore? So he insists, and not that he's slothful — he *grows*, and that, in his words, *takes a lot out of you*. Who needs money if money is hair? — you should hear him say that. I wish you could seal a voice up into an envelope, stamp it, lick it, lick it, lick it, and mail it into an ear slot. You earned money by work and now you earn hair by existence — it's work too, I'll tell you, in this heat . . . but sometimes the work can be forgotten — that's what I'm doing at the Town Hall.

It'll be months until your papers come through — so comb out your lice (Public Enemy #1), brush yourselves to Sunday, and start amassing! Accumulate sacks of it! — in pillow cases, in water glasses, between false book covers. Shave your daughters bald! There's a pleasant waitress here now — almost bald — she just put a down-payment on an above-ground swimming pool (she lives in Joisey, with the horses), if you even know what that is, and I'd be surprised.

Your wives need to be bald! Your dogs, bald — stray dogs, bald. Shave your neighbor's horse if he isn't inclined — ask first, maybe. Stuff your houses with hair, mountains upon mountains. Shave yourselves — don't presume to request sacrifices of everyone else and let your own hair grow free, Father. No, set an example worthy of the head of the household. Grow nine full beards this winter, while your papers are being processed. You're lucky — your hair grows fast. Here my hair has been slowing — the climate is not as conducive here to growth as it is there — slowing even with all this water I'm drinking, or maybe it's not water, but it tastes like nothing, but maybe that's because I've had enough of it or not enough . . . slowed growth from the heat and so you see, there are some benefits, or many ironies, involved with living there . . . here.

(I'm sorry this is sloppy, I'm sloppy, but writing on the bar's a difficult promise and the three different inks here are no code — just the waitress' pens keep giving out.)

The week before your departure, pack it all in large valises — the limit, I believe, for Customs, is nine, and two trunks, enough for a more than modest start. Do you think this strange? The answer, I say, is probably no. Keep on thinking — what would seem strange to us?

So, packed, leave! Request any relatives and friends remaining behind, those with no intention to immigrate, to dutifully shave, often if possible, and to send you, in inconspicuous wrapping, as to avoid theft, their earnings — their harvest which is without season, perpetual. And no need Mother and Father, I have enough — worry about yourselves. Here, enclosed, I send you some of mine, some hair, to get you started — it won't be stolen, no . . . when Layer Man's done sharpening his knife . . . In return you, once here, should send those at home money, precious metals, jewels — I'll send some with my next letter, I promise. Immigration won't ask many questions — the government loves the influx hair. Bribe them with a few strands and they'll act like your cousins, which they might be by then — so many of our countrymen have found their way here, and are all happy and working at excellent jobs, growing immense beards like in the fairy tales I haven't forgotten and often tell Layer Man, who's always very interested.

R. asks about this thing called the *stock market*, which was once a market in which you would purchase imaginary parts of imaginary wholes, imaginary strands of imaginary heads, I know, insane. But now, some advice: now you can buy stock in *real* hair, own shares of someone's hair, a *real* someone, above a neck you can really put your hands around, and now I'm offering you a once in a lifetime opportunity to buy stock in my head. You can own a piece of me. That's some free advice, a *tip* as we say, and take it . . . I can't leave a tip tonight, never do, and you send me money, R., that's how it works, and we'll talk. Aside to R. finished.

Leave that small village, middle of nowhere, and you know why. They're reading this letter now, aren't they? Hello Postal Employees of the State, how are you this fine shorn afternoon? Or maybe not.

You'll not only get a room and a meal. You aren't fools to listen to me. No escaping rooms you'd taken under false pretenses, escaping by a rickety fire escape that just at that moment decides to detach itself from the façade of the building crumbling, no! Falling clutching falling layers, crumbling . . . Leg torn. No, we're not interested. Pain when sitting, standing, walking and lying. No, understandably puzzled, no! Fever and the man with the animal pills. No telling your foolishness, rank stupidity, your plight to a fellow immigrant from a neighboring town, a man I'd met at a laundromat — no laughing — he hadn't been told the same thing, but something far more fanciful . . . And no going insane from cold and hunger, no! And then dying of the heat like desire without Helga there, or her occupied with Mister — but Mother, I don't know anything about that, only rumors . . . O J . . . !

Only the ever-replenishing resource — how could it be worth anything? It is, it is, it is.

A man, an ingenious man, a man of many layers, advising me to go to a wig store and sell my lot. And, after pricing a few, sold to a wide-eyed wig-salesman a family's worth of hair, *fine hair*, he said, *well taken care of* — it fetched almost a hundred. No one spreading gossip here, no! Not in this open letter to be posted in the Town Square or nailed on St. Nicholas' wide iron door like one of their religious tracts . . . which are as false as this is true.

I've been here now for three and a half months — this you *know*. All the rumors you've heard are true, because here, *everything* is true — there's no disabuse of your notions. Prior to your request for the appropriate documents and permissions, commence your growing. Shave and save, clip and snip every strand — this is imperative. The more hair you have, the richer you'll be. Layer Man with his knife stuck into the bar, his tongue in the waitress's ear, I wait.

Build a hair bridge over to this side and avoid the price of passage — walk on your thick strands, hair so strong it'll never give. Yes, I suggest the erection of a locked span across the great water — the ocean I'm sweating and no, Mother, don't worry, I'm not sick, not quite.

(O Mother, I miss you, but I'm, maybe, well, and this was emphatically not a mistake and that's not my pride.)

I've a lock of your hair, Mother, I'll never sell, in a locket, on a necklace, around my neck, near to my heart. Posting this letter will cost me 1 cm. of a head strand or ½ a cm. of a hair strand if my hair was red — which it's not . . . I haven't changed *that* much. I'm closing my eyes and gritting my teeth and focusing only on pumping out this hair, shooting it through these follicles and out into the world, and . . . I must go . . . a white sink bloodstained, dye # whatever and a woman whose purse I snatched yesterday on 5th Avenue wearing my hair on her head, snatched it only after I noticed, I know . . . Layer Man waving me over with the sharpened knife. And the Town Hall's closing and I need to find somewhere else to spend the night that's almost over, even night for you over there, that's how late, St. Nicholas' bells ringing, nostrils, large braided clappers of hair . . . Layer Man's prepared and I must go to him.

I'll dream for us all, until we wake, together, on the other side. Until then, here's my whole head, for you, to save.

Love and *sincerely*,

YOUR SON

THE QUORUM, OR A REPORT TO AN ACADEMY

You, Academy, once failed to understand the sun and now your understanding of the sun is nearly perfected, shaped, and so understand me now, me like the sun, always, turning myself around and around on this one *thing* and thankfully going nowhere, unwavering, maintaining my position, not out of ego or stubbornness but out of essentiality, out of purpose. You, Academy, ignored my light. You, Academy, attempted to keep all in darkness like in that tunnel and round room on the mountain. Even you, Academy, are unable to stop the sun from rising. You, Academy, will only deny I rose.

And as there is one sun, there is one Quorum, or as many Quorums as there are suns, or there are many Quorums who are all the one Quorum. There were ten of them in that specific Quorum or sub-Quorum or sub-sub-Quorum etc., and the Quorum was one of them, which is to write: there weren't ten and the one was made up of the ten that weren't, that never were. And that was the Quorum.

And it was for that statement: *the one Quorum was made up of the ten Quorums that never were . . .* why did I mumble that at the hearing? That was when you, Academy, shut down, right? Yes, I've read the infallible transcript and it was something to that effect. But why even think that thought of mine? Why the idea, how and where from? It was for falling that out of my mouth, in that overheated room in late spring, it was for ending my prepared statement with that which I intended to suppress out of misguided loyalty, and which I anyway expressed so awkwardly, unprepared, there that day: *and the one Quorum was made up of the ten* . . . and for proving this and myself again and again in private meetings with my advisors and the deans to you, Academy, that I was outcast, library privileges revoked. And feeling suddenly over, I returned to the mountain, the place of all this, to live with myself, renting out the old laboratory with money my mother pays me to keep away and starting fires with rags that were once their uniform, strips of striped overalls. This is my report, unprofessional and untainted, to you, Academy.

And so what's it to you, Academy, if I treated and still treat the one as if it was ten, individually, the ten who were one who within itself, within the one, was differentiated and diffuse? Some were fat, some lean, some had hunted and some had gathered. Doctor I numbered them, their identities withheld for purposes of anonymity, to keep the study impersonal and scientific . . . at least that was his initial rationale. The hidden idea, maybe repressed, subconscious, was directed at the mass, was to humiliate the Quorum, deprive it and them of any identity, large or small. However, I preserved some of their waiver forms, the forms that were forced upon them, and list here the first names, ages, sexes, occupations and odd personal details they provided, all of which should be understood as the situations of their perceived individual existences at the date and time at which they were aware of entering the study. For all I know now they, together, were immortal . . . no more. I'll refer to them numerically after, which is how you, Academy, would require it. All were numbered in the order of their initial observation in the field, months prior to their awareness, months prior to my involvement, months prior to the mountain.

One was named Herman, male and a tailor, age 56 and suffering from glaucoma and heart disease, enjoyed numismatics. Two was a manufacturer of women's gloves, name of Nathan, male aged 45, avid player of racquet games. Three was a lawyer, male aged 32, name I forget and his handwriting is illegible, entertained plans of retiring from the practice of law and owning and operating a small seaside hotel. Four was female, age 29, a prostitute, survivor of three abortions, who would attend up to the same number of films per day. Five was an official in the postal service, female aged 38, mother of five, a recovering alcoholic. Six was a rabbi, male aged 89, respected scholar. Seven was a 36-year-old male, an encyclopedia salesman who was addicted to roulette, two sons. Eight was a homemaker, female aged 43, three daughters, two sons, active as a fundraiser for a local zoo. Nine was a retired furrier, male aged 83, swam every day, three children, nine grandchildren. Ten, male aged 34, was a part-time janitor on state support, autistic (though this element of his existence he did not perceive). This is an initial account, flawed — surely as they revolved traits they revolved traces of prior identities and even numbers, and anyway it was difficult to keep it all straight up there. And to answer another question: one man and only him restrained ten entities, or restrained one stronger one, and could only restrain them if they or it was willing to be restrained . . . but they were only willing for a slow season.

Three and Four were the jokers. Doctor I, a man who I at first held in awe, poked Three and Four with heated iron rods and iced their prominent genitals (Three and Four for a significant period of time at a late stage in the study possessed two traits which the others did not: a sense a humor and pro-creative organs), and all three rolled and laughed. The other eight, or the $^8/_{10}$ remainder of the one whole, spent the duration of this experiment writhing in pain, and so it was obvious from the first that we were dealing with a field or group sense.

Academy: if with your permission I may digress and insert a few observations regarding dating. The phenomenon of the Quorum is not a recent development. Doctor I often hypothe-sized whether his discovery of the initial Quorum was actually the Quorum itself, whether it was an idea that he manifested, and in that notion were the first intimations of his insanity. How he tagged them and tracked them months before they were forced to the mountain and all that, in his formulation not to substantiate or weigh his idea, no . . . but to give his idea flesh. You, Academy, should not make myths about his end.

They were one organism — I attest to that — as far apart as they needed or wanted to be, but one . . . despite everything, one. And no, it was not as simple as one was the liver and Seven the heart and Six the spleen, no. You, Academy, must widen your minds — widen your throats like snakes to swallow, and poison, this definition: emotions and socialized activity, every-thing non-tangible, non-ticking and non-fluid producing, everything that would evade the scalpel, functioned as organs, as invisible organs, a metaphysical anatomy. Emotions could become infirm and die. Ideas could become crippled. I realized this only after I returned here, only after I discovered another Quorum, a Quorum of a distinct, group-specific subsistence functioning — I am aware of them and that is all you, Academy, will ever know. They live together, never more than a few lengths apart, as if they're webbed together with invisible, incredibly strong twine — maybe this is because they are, or seem, injured. There are thirty-six here and one has a shattered leg and another is missing a thumb and another is without a nose. It requires all thirty-six of them to assemble all the movable parts of an intact human. It requires two, the two that date or time responsible for one hand each, to open a jar.*

---

*Three further, silent, notes on a possibly related Quorum, to myself:

It was observed that a member with only one arm, example, begets with another member with only one leg, members then of opposite sexes, begets a child (called that for convenience) with one arm and one leg, two limbs, arm and leg on opposite sides of the torso (right arm, left leg, example), and that that member, if its mate has an equal or greater number of anatomical parts, begets another child with even more anatomical parts, increasing incrementally, up to the normal number. These were, mate dependent, generations of an evolving species: a Quorum made up of one member's arm, another's leg, another's head, etc. The only anatomical part that proved a given in all were the reproductive organs — for some reason, each set of reproductive organs were the sole domain of the individuals they were attached to.

Also, an "adult" always seemed part "child" and vice versa — a mental, or intellectual, distinction.

. . . and what exactly determines the makeup of a Quorum? Necessity — and how is necessity determined? Is a Quorum made of a required sum or of the sum available, eligible . . . or evident? And available, eligible or evident when? Does any assemblage make a Quorum, or only if the assemblage individually equals (or exceeds?) a requirement? And the most important questions I, not you, Academy, must ask: what is the requirement and why is it? How is it determined and who exactly does the determining? Unquestionably not you, Academy, not anymore . . .

Academy: I have some questions of my own and I will ask them. I am standing high up at the lectern now and you, Academy, as one, sitting in that lecture hall seat, springs noising around, with you, Academy, sweating. Did you, Academy, not assign me to him and him to me? Answer me. Prior to that I was a research assistant without anyone to assist, and occasionally I was an assistant to an assistant. I was useless — you, Academy, know that — it's on file. I was an errand runner, a messenger, a finder of facts and a filler of halls and seats, sitting through lectures so the echoes they would have something undead to hit and return from. Then you, Academy, assigned me, instructed me to report to such and such an office on the specified day at the time of your setting. Is this not true, not on record and verifiable? Why someone like me, a non-distinguished paired with someone who was thought of among the faculty's greatest minds? What mistake put me on what list and whose mistake was it? Do you, Academy, rotate fault, share, and if so, how equally? On the initial interview Doctor I sat across from me, hands on my knees, paternal, and outlined his aims and theories.

Academy: didn't this assignment require my devotion, my softer qualities and is that why? Were you not, in your *loco parentis* and as per the forms I happily signed and rights which reverted, my proxy assent to all this madness? Like you, Academy, I ask everything rhetorically. Important to acknowledge that I was an assistant, a specialist, albeit a specialist in a specialty that would be impossible to train for and even more impossible to become qualified in. I was merely an introduced element. An early winter into my relationship with Doctor I and he had diagnosed me as the equalizer or unifier for this particular Quorum. He thought of me as his son and I at first had no objections. And soon you, Academy, funded the mountain laboratory and reimbursed me for the train ticket up there in deep winter and I have the receipt here with me somewhere, in the same room where it all happened, unless I used it in a fire to keep warm.

That first night I arrived on the mountain, over a poor dinner of plain noodles, Doctor I explained to me his method. Unable to accurately trace the passage of responsibilities and traits, he was despondent — his government grant was nearly exhausted and you, Academy, were already having your doubts, am I right? I was to be introduced into the Quorum as a member, my purpose to record how the others reacted to this development. I was instructed to imitate and trade traits, within guidelines and tables, to receive from others their influence and to attempt to pass on and instigate in the others specific habits, mannerisms and reactions. I would fake and would they find me out and isn't that the outline of my whole endeavor so far? Would they sense my foreignness and ignore me, or would they adapt to me or destroy me or what? Those were the questions which were one question. I and that question underlying me were to be introduced soon.

You, Academy, asked me at the hearing to describe the underground laboratory prior to its destruction that night, and I will, sitting here in the small house, above the guts I've made no effort to rebuild. The front porch of the house, then, in the winter, filled with snow, led into the small one room, the personal quarters of Doctor I, a room and a washroom in one, both of which out of necessity I shared with him. A trapdoor set in the floor, down a spiral staircase, led to the underground tunnel, the laboratory, a tunnel lined with unfurnished rooms behind heavy wooden doors, a prison with ten inmates and their warden and who was I? The members of the Quorum or sub-Quorum etc. were each kept in their own room, locked in, with no plumbing or ventilation, or light. They were taken out for experiments in the large round room at one end of the tunnel and the other end it was filled in with rubble, long ago, I must think, an old mine shaft. Immediately prior to them being taken out to the room, which happened once a day, they were sedated. The smell and sounds down there were unbearable: feces and screaming, imprecations and urine — everything was damp and overgrown with fungi and mold. Those of the Quorum who at a date and time were responsible for eating subsisted on mushrooms which grew from the walls.

Of my group, of the group of Doctor I, Eight and Ten were initially significantly obese. A week later, Two and Seven were obese to the same degree. Eight had developed a skin irritation and Ten darkened, the melanin in its system, according to the diagnosis of Doctor I, tripling in an afternoon. These differences notwithstanding, Eight and Ten seemed nearly related, sometimes, in their facial structures. When Eight fell down in the round room, after a whipping, Ten, in its room, was evidently assigned the pain. When One, who during this particular late afternoon observation seemed to be female, touched Ten, Eight salivated uncontrollably. One and Seven ate for them all for three days straight while the others fasted. We soon learned the passage of traits was not one to one. One to three was possible, two to seven was not unusual, and partial passage was observed in many instances. Also, as in the salivating response, a reaction would often be provided by a third party seemingly uninvolved in any one-on-one interaction.

Something happened in the early spring. Nine, from seeming oblivion, began singing in Italian (did any of them know Italian?), opera excerpts (did any of them know opera?), Mozart and Verdi most of all, in a luminous mezzo-soprano. Nine was now a woman, the only one of the ten in the one. Doctor I thought that their particular state of exclusive hermaphroditism (and occasional asexuality) on any given day or time was a factor of whim and situation, not of necessity. Anyway, while I listened and Doctor I thought, Nine sang, excerpts, then full roles. No one else or no other element had ever sung before and that week neither the inclination nor the talent passed — we thought it possible that they would pass separately, though we would never have known if only the talent had passed, so that part of that experiment was never resolved. We waited for a longer assimilation period and we waited longer and nothing happened.

And so Doctor I began a search for the larger Quorum, the group of which this Quorum was to be merely a sub-Quorum. He was extending everything — didn't you, Academy, recognize the mania in him? Everything larger, ever larger, meaning more and implicating further and speculating further and imagining infinitely, all unsound, in every direction, at once. He was pursuing links, relationships in actions and emotions, ever finer relationships, more and more elusive and illusory, in his own head — he was insane and I was afraid. And besides my fear, how was I doing, how was my introduction into the Quorum turning out? Not very well — no matter what I did, no matter how audacious or mundane, and though all of it was planned for maximum effect, I was ignored, and I attributed this failure or the failure of the Quorum, not my failure, to the madness of Doctor I, but was I right to?

But for an answer could I have turned to you, Academy? Certainly not. And to pass on my fears? Turned to you, Academy, to libel a star scientist, a valued member of the learned faculty, and me, who was I, an assistant? No. One evening after our regular dinner of noodles I drafted a letter to you, Academy, detailing my misgivings and you, Academy, now have the only copy in your files and I can only access it from memory and yet it is my letter — it's dated April 1, isn't it? Doctor I read it as I slept and his aloud reading of it woke me up and we locked heads. He was about to leap when the trapdoor smashed open. We had not heard the destruction below us, not heard possibly because we were not willing to hear.

I understand and appreciate only in retrospect that the Quorum's revolt was immaculately planned except for one unknown: the pistol. Somehow free from their rooms, they ambushed Doctor I as he was ambushing me. How did they get free, you, Academy, questioned me for hours on this and I didn't know and still don't. Doctor I reached for his pistol, which he always slept with, loaded, under his pillow on his mattress across from where I lay, and he shot Three, not three of them, but number Three, now the largest and about to strangle. I shut my eyes, shut all my senses and stayed lying still.

Three lay there in the middle of the room with a sucking

wound and within an hour was dead. The other members of the Quorum . . . they didn't disappear — they didn't age quickly and turn to dust as I have since imagined (yes, I now imagine) — they just weakened, slowly weakened, lay on the mattress of Doctor I, leaned against the walls of the room and the doorway, slumped down, their knees at their lips, and submitted through the long night. Some physically separated themselves along the porch to suffer alone, possibly in an attempt to save some of them or it, a severing of limb to keep alive everything else sacrifice, but this effort only made them mesh tighter, together. They shuddered and grew limp, lay fetal and I was there, awake and helpless and senseless on my mattress as they ignored me — as they died into the morning, into the sun's rising. I had underestimated their level of dependency. In the morning, there were one and ten dead.

Instead of attending the funeral of Doctor I (a decision incredibly held against me at my hearing), I was at home, in the room I had when I was young, while my mother sat in silence downstairs. A long month later I returned to the Academy, to interrogations and reviews and the hearing scheduled the week before exams, and then silence. And I would not, as you, Academy, already know, file a report in line with your instructions — I would not outline my observations and experiments and ignore the other proofs. You, Academy, trained me too well and I didn't want to disappoint, to set a poor example. You, Academy, would have found such a report lacking, and you, Academy, are too sacred to insist on such false specifications, am I right? What is it that you, Academy, are so afraid of?

Whatever it is, you, Academy, asked me to take a leave of

absence and not take my exams, not finish the term and then you, Academy, declined to renew my enrollment for the fall. And so not knowing what to do, and my mother afraid of me and not wanting me home, I returned to the mountain, rented the laboratory from the state and the first labor I applied myself to was the writing of this report, less scientific and yet more honest than you wanted, written on the porch in the pure snow. Rigor abandoned me, not the other way around and knowing that you, Academy, ignorantly know freedom only as the opposite of rigor, I offer you my following thoughts:

Perhaps the Quorum was part of a larger Quorum, from whom they'd wandered astray and further, perhaps they are all of a single Quorum, not injured — only dwindling, slowly and unknowingly. This is the large thinking of Doctor I, however my large thinking is not grand but sad . . . as they or it is all dying forever and yet will never die out, never extinct. It's another one of my unlinked ideas that the Quorum is not organized as a simultaneity, that the Quorum, as it exists in time and in space, in a far-flung reach of events and ideas in the present and on maps, should also exist *through* time and *through* space. Such an idea postulates a hierarchy of effects traceable to an origin — a God maybe . . . a lineage of actions and equal and opposite reactions and that idea seems acceptable, if only for the exercise. However I also like to think that members of the Quorum are merely willing participants in the more humane experiment of reincarnation, although in the spiritual sense only — that something of someone, a feeling, a memory, presents itself to another for no reason understandable, to either party . . . and that this reincarnation *is* the Quorum. It's not that nothing is lost in this system or anti-system of reincarnation, it's that nothing is denied its initial existence — this is what justifies this idea to me, this *responsible* idea.

I'll never know and I'll never prove anything to you, Academy, though late at night into early morning I have begun to sense other things — the tiredness of a young girl, example, the longing of an old, old man — living through me, and it's only then that I exhale and forget the specifics, all of which, nothing more and nothing less, I have adumbrated for you, Academy, despite having no responsibility to do so, here.

HESSH'S BEDS

How, Doctor, to introduce myself? I ran here. My problem? If you're ready, I'll begin with the word. Though I won't pronounce well, excuse and indulge me. It's my hour that's not really an hour I'm paying one-hundred-fifty dollars for, isn't it? This is all the truth, and the truth is — the truth in *this language*, a language which almost encourages its speakers to lie — the truth is that I've forgotten how to form the word, the letters, their lines . . . the placement of tongue in mouth, to the palate, the glottal whatever . . . I never kissed him, Doctor, I never even kissed him.

At home — with what you're charging your home must be a remarkable specimen of fat and happiness — at home, you have beds. From where? Who'd you buy off of? Not from Hessh, then, good, Doctor. I just wanted to make sure. You went to the place out by that Mandarin restaurant? You probably paid too much.

And anyway, my description of the word would just be an excuse for your inattention . . . my description of it to myself, a mental description, is just an excuse, or a rationale, for my absent memory, or my unforgivable, and inexplicable, inattentiveness while in his presence. Please, Doctor, don't do me the same disservice. He, Hessh, Doctor, was so focused on you, so intent, and I haven't felt anything since, though it's only been a week, and now I feel . . . How should I describe, Doctor? I should lie down.

I am lying down.

Though his language was an indictment of description, it didn't forsake description — his language reserved its descriptive resources for the most mundane situations. I, Doctor, must ineptly transgress.

Transliterated, this word in the nameless language — this word which describes in one of our nouns the involved situation and act which brought us together — this word, Doctor, would be something like: *yodsheyngaiyltenden*, maybe, though if you'd pronounced it like that, no one would understand you. There were no near-phonetic allowances in their understanding, nor any near-phonetic humorous mistakes — inexactitude meant, was, pure failure. Its language is now dead. And its last speaker, my friend Hessh, is dead too. I miss him, Doctor, miss him terribly.

Yodsheyngaiyltenden, untranslatable in one word, means, roughly: *engaging-in-sexual-intercourse-with-a-person-on-the-bed-you-sell-him-or-her* — a strange practice, strange to us at least, and Hessh's specialty. Hessh's first name, transposed to our language, would be Adam, name of the first man, the man whose task it was to name things, though it's never recorded who, or what, named him. And Hessh was the last, Doctor. This act, this *yodsheyngaiyltenden*, was not our first intimacy . . . Our first was when he asked me where my wife was, and I explained I had none, when he asked where my fiancée or girlfriend was, and I explained I had none, when he asked how many pillows I used, and it amazed him that I wasn't sure, when he asked what position I favored in sleep, and I explained that I didn't know. How was I supposed to know? I asked him, I was asleep, to which he smiled his incredible smile, such a white, natural, enormous smile, and laughed.

He was the last, Doctor, I promise, no more after him.

He was a man of another world, of other values, and his world moved with him. His open sky never got roofed in with faux shingles, the ones above my head — they came with the house, and the house had come with the job, and I'd come here, to this wasteland from years of wasted utopia studying economics, for both. I worked in the advertising industry, Doctor, too many years. I sold people ideas for selling things to people, themselves, ourselves . . . I, Doctor, like you, am worthless.

This Adam, my Hessh, was a bed salesman, Doctor, *the* bed salesman if you ask around at trade fairs and industry get-togethers . . . and it *is* a hermetic industry. Bed salesmen, and they're mostly sales*men*, tend towards obesity and jealousy — they'd whisper, if you asked around, about Hessh, in awe. They weren't jealous of Hessh — he was death for them. Feared, and yet harmless. His existence was historically, intellectually perfect, and yet, in all other apprehensions, not so. Unable to be ignored, Doctor, and yet not demanding anything from anyone, Hessh the Bed King, predictably, they called him. Hessh was always quick to remark that there were no kings in his language, and so not in his kingdom, which then wasn't, accurately, a *kingdom* — the word with most *give* (as mattresses are described) with regard to *king*, in his language, was a word I forget, however the meaning was something like: *man-whom-God-asks-politely-to-believe-in-Him*. Yes, Doctor, there was a God in Hessh's world, however this God was as harmlessly foolish as the men who swarmed around Hessh at the unveilings of new product lines, men who engaged him in earnest relationships, sealed with sweaty handshakes. These men — into mattresses, frames, headboards which attached to the wall, bunks, canopies, daybeds, waterbeds, trundles, sofa fold-outs and pull-outs, obsolete Murphys, whoever he was, orthopedic adjustables, everything — knew the jargon, spoke the assuming language of next-generation spring-tension or whatever and beyond and yet failed to understand the meaning. They sold lidless coffins and dream-repositories, understand, and they understood only technological advances pertaining to the support of the lower lumbar spine.

Doctor, what these greased men lacked was tradition, aspirations beyond their own meager perfections as salesmen and lodge-members and husbands and fathers and organized-sports fanatics. Hessh's great-grandfather had been a leading member of the bed salesman caste, a leading caste (directly under, and sometimes marrying into, the caste of clergy) in the now nonexistent Kingdom of x, a place he described to me, in his own language, as *sh'amay*, meaning *there*, apparently a term of great praise.

How should I know?

My friend Hessh, Doctor . . . what there was to know about selling beds, he knew, and how to sell, he also knew. You walked in wanting a modest twin, say, and you left with a queen, or a deluxe round rotating waterbed with same-sized ceiling-mounted mirror. Ordinary hospital white sheets you wanted, now red, silk, with matching pillows and down comforter.

Bedding them, congressing his customers, Doctor . . . sex was not part of his sales routine. (He never stained the mattresses — he flipped them over only with a thought to equal wear on the merchandise.) The act, the sexual act, was an act of courtesy, it was considered, from the days before there were springs to noise around and disrupt focus, in his great-grandfather's days of fabric sewn around straw, it was considered an act of *courtesy* . . . just as Morris, the baker down the strip, adds a thirteenth to a dozen. I go out of my way to buy his bread and rolls . . . from his window I can see Hessh's old shop, what's now a laundromat, one of the very few around I don't use, to keep my whites white, and won't.

I own a sedan, Doctor, but I often run, and when I don't run, I lie.

To seduce and to sell was not a victory, but an act of goodwill, of neighborliness, though many suspecting husbands didn't understand it as such. But through sheer humanity, Hessh remained alive and intact. The husbands would arrive, wielding pipes or baseball bats or crowbars, be invited in for tea, expertly steeped tea, and leave, an hour or so later, having made a new friend.

Am I tiring you? Should I go on? I'm tiring myself . . .

His, Hessh's, was a light sell, Doctor. Inside the strip-mall exterior, the storefront along a major route joining the suburbs with the urbis, inside the storefront under the Hessh's Beds sign — a sign as direct and unassuming as the store's proprietor . . . But once inside the door — his private showroom, a sanctum by appointment only, his home too, where *he* slept, a harmless infraction of zoning laws — but I will not *describe* . . . allow me only to invoke low lighting, mild fruity incense, soul music sung, as he put it, by the *descendants of slaves*. His family was itself enslaved immediately prior to the genocide.

Doctor, I remember his even speech in his third language, my language, ours, in his light x-accent offering me to *try it out*, and patting the mattress lovingly — such neatly manicured hands. And his smell, talcum — a masculine man, a man who knew how to provide, effortlessly, for his own appearance and satisfaction, and had no embarrassment for it. A man who was elegant in his exertions, elegant even when he sweated.

Many succumbed to him, Doctor — he was attractive, how couldn't they? A last of his kind, sole survivor of the holocaust of x a generation ago — how could he be refused? Submission to Hessh was as much a certainty as his customers' ignorance of his past, his people. But they didn't submit out of pity — at least I speak for myself. Hessh, the last tribe member, carrying on the tradition of bed salesmanship handed down from generation to generation . . . He'd explain this tradition to his mostly moneyed suburban customers, lonely housewives looking to remodel their bedrooms, looking to trash the set they'd bought with their husbands, or were gifted, for their wedding nights — when they had less to dispose of incomewise . . . husband paying off law school loans, working incredible hours . . . He'd hear their stories too, Doctor, these various, preordained traditions of ascent . . . did I say *tradition*, Doctor?

I hate my language.

And when the women left his, Hessh's, presence, Doctor, their aches didn't ache anymore, no more complaints of cramping, soreness or stiff neck.

Not one woman he slept with, Doctor, who didn't purchase a bed — some purchased three or four, more than they intended, needed, more beds than they had bedrooms for . . .

and did they ever have bedrooms! in these stately pastel manses. After the initial encounter, he never made house calls. This was an art, tradition, not the preying it might seem. And he lost his life last week, Doctor — a heart attack, an attack of the heart — in the act, in the heat of his exertions, atop a dyed blonde, late 40s, early 50s. He collapsed and died atop her . . . him, the last speaker of this beautiful language.

And now I'm here. Having run here, I'll run home.

And so, Doctor, the language died too, and with it, the acts and emotions it codified and communicated. There were many — how to put it? — *concepts* in this language, nonexistent as concepts now, only associations among often unrelated words. The word in our language *last*, had no equivalent in Hessh's. So is it true, his lastness? The only things that exist are those that exist *in language*. But many women had children by him, Doctor. The blood of x lives on in dark-haired children — where else did the neighborhood children get these features from? Come down my block any day after school lets out, Doctor, come under the wide-spaced oaks and watch these children at play, these swarthy children, all brothers and sisters. They're alive, very much so, almost too alive, but the language, the language of their father, is certainly dead.

I, myself, a longtime customer, *the most loyal*, he said, I, a man, know — for my ten beds, six of which he sold me at cost — I know only four or five words, and each one is remarkable.

He often remembered to me his early years, Doctor, years apprenticed to various relatives, learning the fundamentals of sales and seduction. A family maxim: a sale is as much a lifeless transaction as each party allows it to be. To some, Doctor, yes, it's a slow seduction, a union of desires. He remembered to me the invasions, the destruction of the libertine life to which his people were accustomed, a lifestyle mandated, and then the destruction of the people themselves. How he escaped, sewn into a mattress by his father, the finest mattress, his father's own, confiscated by the high commander of N, seized. How he could hardly breathe except through a small hole his father ripped, painfully. How he endured three nights inside, below the sexing and fitful sleep of the victorious general and his slavegirls, three of whom were Hessh's sisters, Doctor, above. The escape, the jump out the window, down a rope of tied sheets, into the moat and out, the wandering, vagabonding, a refugee . . . and the slow realization that he was the last, the only survivor of the 10,000-plus of his people. A people of admirably preserved traditions, strange-to-us decorum. A people of a phenomenal, ineffable language, a language without a word for itself. A rough, sexual, masculine language. A profound language, Doctor. A language that didn't encompass tenses — the past was the future, all expressed in what we would know of as the *present*. A language in which, he said, *it is impossible to lie*.

Are you listening, Doctor? Were you? Will you more?

He talked in his sleep, Doctor: *t'sheventeiyd*, meaning: *a-prenatal-forgiveness-for-all-sins-a-child-commits-in-his-or-her-lifetime*. The language also knows no gender. *G'vikeiyn* meaning: *a-cheese-aged-to-be-coeval-with-the-age-of-an-eldest-relative*, a rare and coveted delicacy. *Todahbahkeytodahbah* meaning: *I-thank-you-because-I-truly-feel-thankful-and-not-because-social-norms-compel-me-to-thank-you*. This last he has said to me often, awake and asleep, together and in dream, and I return the word to him, in my mind, if I may. He was gentle with me — it was my first time with a man, and my last. He let me attempt him first and then, when we assured each other of my pleasure, Doctor, we switched. And I have not sought any embrace since, with any sex, and I do not think I will, Doctor, but it has only been a week.

Do you have any water?

A question presents itself and so let's sell it an answer, Doctor: when is a language the largest, if by largest we mean the most variegated, the most flexible, the richest, multitudinous? What do you think? when it's spoken by the most people or when it's spoken by the least? well? I would opt for the latter, the least. Though large numbers of people will evolve any number of dialects, slang, etc., only a generation, or a family, or a couple, or an individual, can evolve such a personal system of jokes and references, at once incomprehensible to strangers and also . . . deep. And another one I know, Doctor: *eeshlonekoneshaiyn'avalheiym* . . . and it stretches out further, the whole thing meaning: *it's-amazing-how-few-men-purchase-beds-these-days-but-those-who-do-are* . . . I forget the rest. I forget his word, his one word, for that, for me. I was his first and only man on this side of the ocean (he said, and I must believe), and he was mine, my last.

I've always lived alone, Doctor, preferred it. Can you tell? The first bed he sold me at a handsome discount — he never took advantage of anyone — it was delivered, by his staff of illegal immigrants, Asians he afforded opportunity. It's lasted for almost a decade, and I flip the mattress every year as per

his instructions, and, no, not funny, I've never torn off the tags
. . . Yes, I know you didn't ask . . .

Doctor, I have assembled all the beds he ever sold me — it took me ho urs and assaulted my groin and knees — assembled them in my largest room, what I would refer to as the *dining room*, if I was in the habit of naming rooms, of naming anything, except my losses. Doctor, this is now a room of beds, of one enormous bed, sex-high. To enter the room one must step up from the doorway, onto the bed, no shoes allowed.

It's hard for me to leave, and if I do it's only to run, to the bakers (crumbs on the beds, pitiful), to the bank, the laundromat, the necessary things, to here, now, understand? I've tried to write this down . . . can you believe our language, Doctor, still exists on paper? finitely and relatively unalterably? Are you taking notes?

Only in that bedroom, my enormous bedroom (though I don't call it that), do I take off my running shoes — shoes with a special heel designed to lessen the impact of the hard world on my soft being. I take them off (they have no laces), and I roll around on the beds. Beds pushed up against each other and the walls. I roll and roll and roll and roll, howling and pushed out again when I hit the walls.

I'll sell my sedan, my *roomy sedan* the salesman said, and pull all the shades in my too-large house — the neighbors have been watching, Doctor.

Yes, I understand, my time is up and I'll pay . . . because you, or, more accurately, your services, are not covered by my insurance, Doctor. How do you sleep at night? Not very funny, Doctor . . . Should I pay you? No, your assistant . . . The payment, I must assume, itself therapeutic. I'll sign my name to a check. Paid to the order of Doctor Feinberg, right? I can spell it, Doctor. A check for the ultimately untranslatable sum of one-hundred-fifty dollars.

And then I'll run home, Doctor, to beds.

We are mothers to history. The raising of history is our responsibility, a responsibility we're born into. But we understood this only after we were taken in.

If we fail in our responsibility, fail to engender, then all of history is merely a fleeting, one-night encounter, a virgin encounter (Puah the Fourth), which lasts forever, which may be understood in any manner we awake so deciding, when we awake, after forever.

We sleep much, some more than others, Nina Sleeping most of all.

If we fail in our responsibility, fail to raise history up to the highest altar under a new moon, then history is no one's sacrifice.

Our failure would be what Solomon's people understand as a mortal sin, a sin punishable in death. We exist for our responsibility and our responsibility exists, because we do. We don't exist (Sarah the Ninth, numbered as a king) if we fail.

Anyone is the father of history and he's never allowed more than a hard length from our harem. A man's soft length, says Ila Womb of Wormwood, is the length of his days. Everything inside is soft, outside, hard. Most of us never knew our fathers, but Batya the Olive did and would like to record him here, to leave him here, she says.

Those among us who were born of Solomon's people are our sisters. Solomon's people are a people because they say they are.

Intelligence is the ability to engender a false son, a son

carved from raw ideas, impulses (Batya the Olive), dreams . . . as different as they are many . . . and the ability to make it stand. What is an idea, an impulse, a dream, receives flesh . . . usurpers descending from a personal flaw, says Gesh the Small, the water to the jug to the water in the jug, says the first Nila, the sand to the rock, to sand again. This false son would be what Solomon's people understand as an idol.

Swaddled stone, have I heard? What's your name? Does anyone know her? Ila will call her bones, stillborn . . .

But it's not intelligence we're dealing with, I remind, it's wisdom.

It's tempting to speculate that Solomon's wisdom was great in proportion to the women he kept, to us: the greater the number of women, the greater their diversity — long hair, short hair, large breasts (Dina's the largest), small, black, copper, white, amusing, quiet — the greater the king. A few women (not slaves, Skinny Hagar) purchased or, more regularly, forced into the harem, meant for Solomon new insights, and, more importantly, deeper understandings of inherited ideas.

We are ambassadors from other beliefs.

And so a king, any king — and we've known a few kings, of a few lands — is only an idol, a product of his women's intelligence. A wise king understands that, and Solomon was wise.

But does Solomon realize that his kept women, us, waiting half our lifetimes, it seems, for our turns in the cycle — a cycle much, much longer in duration than the moon's (Lara who Limps), and more palpably felt (Jafen) — does he realize that we keep men of our own? Surely in his great wisdom he would've noticed, taken a break from the clouds and at least thought about it. About our lives without him. About us, says Hind the Dark, when he's not inside us.

Dina, the third Dina, would like to make it known that many of the thoughts expressed above are hers and we've decided in favor of her request. We vote, none of us are kings. Most of us will remain anonymous, necessarily (Dina). Dina's the self-proclaimed intellectual among us. I'm the senior woman, I've known many years, and I've the last eye on this record, as long as I have sight.

The full moon brings our menstruations, we all menstruate together, our houses run with blood. Sand stuck in blood, desert of one infinite grain.

Solomon was hardly out of childhood when David named him, his youngest son, oldest in ability, his successor. Reza Our Elephant remembers nothing about the ceremony, but says the day was unusually cold.

One attribute of intelligence, says Dina, of an intelligent person, is the unfortunate tendency to miss things, mundane things, going on around him, to be distracted by intellectual pursuits. One attribute of wisdom, says Dina, of a wise person, is the ability to affirm that these mundane things don't matter much, a willed ignorance that allows the wise to focus on higher matters, more weighty truths.

Solomon must know, for example, that the Queen of Sheba keeps other men, doesn't live for him. He knows this as he knew the answers to her questions. He knew the questions before they were asked and we knew the answers before they existed.

Solomon thought himself wise, wiser than Ethan the Ezrahite, Heman, Kalcol and Darda, the sons of Mahol.

Mahol was wise for having them. Too many thoughts, one belief. Mahol didn't have them. No one asked them, says Nina Sleeping.

Solomon has three-thousand proverbs, one thousand and five songs. Our musician improvises.

Without a people, a king is as nothing. The kings after Solomon will be as nothing, the kingdom no one's son. But, I remind, we are forbidden from prophecy, dreaming is not prophecy, or not wholly prophecy.

Who knows from Saul? David's Jonathan . . . ? *We've* had arrows, says Jafen, shot in *our* caves.

We are the mothers from generations upon generations past. We've had daughters by Solomon and daughters by men who were not Solomon, and sons. None (Small-Nippled Aya) will be kings.

Imagine, as distant as you might be, columns, curtains billowing, dream, and find yourself peeping into a large, round room: the eunuchs stand, fat and imperious, a man kneeling, plucking on the harp, singing inanities, wafting scents of burning Temple herbs.

Imagine, if you will, the place and circumstances of conception, of this mass record: all of us women, young and old (old meaning young by the standards of the outside world, me), lounging on pillows draped in fine Egyptian linen, pillows as enormous as they are soft, dictating to a eunuch who claims he knows how to write, with Dina, our intellectual Dina, making sure he makes no mistakes and, in his timidity, that he misses nothing, omits not a word. We're a dictating harem, and this emasculated man is our secretary. We thank him, by allowing him to serve.

We're leaving behind this record of our lives, of our independence. Our lives are what we were and what we've made. We're not merely belongings, possessions. *Our* possessions include: thirty-six eunuchs for the three hundred of us at present. Another war, and there'll be more.

Three hundred, and we all need a voice over the music. Our days (Nina Waking) are waiting. Music surrounds us.

We occasionally receive visits from our daughters, it's imperative they remain secrets, never our sons, though they're secrets too. Though Solomon knows, must know, he must not. Solomon tells us each secrets, secrets he says he tells no one else and which he instructs us not to reveal to anyone, state secrets, personal secrets. He tells each of us these secrets, and each of us the instruction not to reveal to anyone. Since we are no one, we reveal them, drinking and laughing, to each other.

We're not whores, we're women. We're the true rulers, says Roni, of this whoredom. Someone I hear under the music and us has been telling the same joke over and over.

Sarah, his favorite, naked, wore his crown once and couldn't hold up her head under its weight. Solomon only wore it when seated.

We all have asked him to shave his beard. He's much more attractive (and softer, Ona Younger Than Ona) without it. He's trimmed it short, to the ridicule of his advisors, and such is our power. We've denied the advisors many times, also visiting kings.

Much of what we remember about our encounters with Solomon have been imagined, or dreamt. Sometimes Solomon appears as his God and sometimes his God appears as Solomon, in dreams.

The sequence of dream-images (we are trained, by Priests, to dream from our arrival in the harem, after our virginal inspection), the dream-sequence easily falls into the trap of history: if you don't seek out relations, links, use your waking intelligence, artfully, you lose any sense of effect, of governance.

We're shouting out ideas over the music, none of us obeying our turns to speak, to testify, to offer something to this record, and now I am hoarse and must gargle honey. We hope our scribe is not too timid to transcribe everything, every detail of our lives, adding nothing of his own, nothing imagined.

How can you imagine without a sex?

We enjoy being oiled and pampered, anointed, bathed and anointed again with herbs and oils from distant lands. Aloe, cinnamon and myrrh perfume our beds, our altars says Fina. Solomon lasts for hours and then some moons he can't maintain an erection at all. Kaya remarks that kings are also anointed.

The music's strange even for music, now: it's heavier, intervals tightly-spaced as if one note was swallowing itself and throwing itself back up again. The musician's tired, but who tired him?

And then a woman *is* always vomiting in the corner, I add, women here are always pregnant. Pregnancy is a form of promotion, we feel we must explain, pregnant women are moved to private quarters and are assigned personal servants, their children will be well taken care of.

Our pregnancy is a public secret. Public secrets, says Dina, are what bring day and night in their own times.

Sarah's one of Solomon's favorites, says Sarah, and no one disagrees. She's dark-haired and dark-eyed (we describe her), the rest of her is phenomenally white. Besides her, Fina says, proudly, Solomon favors the dark ones, black. Sarah speaks seven languages by her own accounting, understands the rudiments of mathematics and poetry. Even so, Dina's the intellectual, Sarah the sensualist. She also refuses to be ordered around: claiming she's an errant granddaughter of David's Batsheva (and so, we enjoy teasing her, Solomon's exiled daughter), she refuses to come when Solomon calls her, coming to him always a night after. Solomon, man that he is, king that he is, understood this and called for her a day before he wanted her, a day before he thought he wanted her. She understood this and for awhile came two nights after she was initially called. Solomon then began calling her two days before, and she came three nights. And the pursuit went on and on, Solomon allowing it, in my opinion, only because of her extreme beauty and tenderness. He would never have tolerated such behavior in any of his other women, in the rest of us, and especially not in his wives.

We're all responsible for a degree of jealousy towards Sarah, Solomon's favorite, Sarah asks us to admit. We're not jealous of the wives, we hate them, *they* are jealous. They seek to own an idol. The musician wishes to add (and we'll dig in our fingernails for his impertinence, and record his insight): idols are never owned, they own.

We've never met the Pharaoh's daughter, Solomon's first wife, though she lives one hundred steps away.

It's time to eat, food is plentiful, we resist. We keep our figures, though, for ourselves. We're weighed, says Kaya, on no honest scales.

Solomon (Garni Eats Orange) has never sliced our children in half.

Our ears are many times pierced, the rings are percussion to the harp when we lie and rise. Bring her one more earring, Lara Who Limps says, and she'll piss through it.

When Solomon married the Pharaoh's daughter, she gifted him a thousand musical instruments and ordered them played in honor of her God, her idol (to Solomon), and Solomon did not forbid her. All you need, says Leah Quiet, is the harp.

When Solomon married the Pharaoh's daughter, it's said an angel named Gabriel descended and planted a reed in the sea, on which a great city is being built. Will we ever visit it? No, only his wives travel with him. Will that city become greater than Jerusalem, so large as to shadow us here? We disagree.

God talked to Solomon and Solomon talked to us, he repeated God's words and they sounded like Solomon's.

This tactic of delay, of anticipation and flirtatious denial, its success, inspired Sarah to announce to Solomon her affection for the musician, whose name she never knew. The musician was bound by order of the king never to address the women and never to answer when addressed. Fearing for his livelihood if not for his life, the musician obeyed. What else to do? After her announcement, the musician disappeared. We don't have to use our imaginations.

All women are worth more than rubies, says Niva with the Scar, but no woman is worth more than one ruby. Give her, I say, an apple of silver peel and golden fruit.

The most of us who have had Solomon at once was one-hundred-and-eight. We had him together for no special occasion, he merely summoned us on an impulse, we know, a moon into the new year. Impulses are signs of weakness, of knowing yourself. Knowing others is far more valuable than knowing yourself, gold to silver, silver to Lebanon cedar. Niva's apple, a pit of Lebanon cedar. After that night into day, we had him one at a time. Hard as Lebanon cedar was Solomon in his youth.

It's time to eat again, says a eunuch, but we don't eat because it's time. Solomon eats at our loaves.

Each of Solomon's thousand wives prepares his dinner in her own house, in the possibility that he may visit that evening. He'll visit each maybe two or three times in their whole lives.

So many and so little time. A thousand of them, wives, like musical instruments, three hundred of us, a fledgling nation. Some of us have never slept with him, but none of us are virgins.

He took in some of us to keep us from other men, to deny them our power. He is jealous as his God.

He's never put one of us to death, or even struck us. We've struck him, however, he asked. Once he asked one of us, we won't record which, to put him to death.

Sarah's slept with him the most: eighteen times. Most have slept with him only once, our virgin time. We weren't that adept, then. Why didn't he have us initiated (Sixth Dina) before he indulged? It would've greatly increased his pleasure.

Dina reports the scribe is performing well, with great accuracy, maybe we'll reward him. But how?

We initiated ourselves, Solomon noticed and he did not.

One whisper in an ear, from Solomon: *Better it is to have no children, and to have virtue: for the memorial thereof is immortal: because it is known with God, and with men.*

THE MEN OF THE WOMEN OF SOLOMON

The musician, now, is one, the son of a prosperous oil merchant another, the son of a man who sells illumination (Gali), the High Priest, believe it or not, is another, and a beggar of whom Beth of One Green Eye and One Blue Eye is fond for reasons none of us, and maybe not even her, understand. Some of us are night-black and some of us are star-white, the rest in between, all the men are men. How we met them is immaterial, forbidden. We forget the particulars in the heart of the act.

Short Leah slept with Hiram of Tyre, and his father, not at once, she had an hour between, during which a eunuch — (they're all nameless, to us at least) — fanned her with palm fronds. Leah says the father was better, but the son enjoyed himself more.

Pleasure, says Tall Leah, is the world in the heart of the act. Before and after, adds Hind the Dark, seem more like dreams.

Surely there are other young men, of certain family, whom we occasionally grant favors, without shame, upon their presentation of appropriate gifts and recommendations: they're young and innocent and tender and we seem old and wise, and tender enough. They're mystics in training and we're realists who dream.

We were all virgins previous to Solomon, we faithfully promise into an ear, we were examined.

Shame, says Red Ina, is their problem, not mine. No rain has fallen in six moons.

Strangely, they enjoy kissing, spend more time kissing when we'd rather get to the heart of the act. Maybe they kiss because they feel they have to: a suggestion of Nin which Rachel the Smile thinks admirable. When we embrace, hairless them, we forget.

Solomon enjoys being on top, lying on your back you can count the stars, I've understood. Rachel the Smile abhors kissing, the taste of any lips besides those of her sisters, when she has other men, she's always on top. Nin smears honey on her breasts for the man who sews the hems of her garments. He can't lick though, she rides him with such fury, the thick honey drips down to his mouth.

Sarah, the twelfth Sarah, of the golden hair, had the musician, not the other way around. Rachel had a eunuch's younger brother and another eunuch's sister, the musician playing louder, us singing, observing in pleasure, to hide any sounds.

But this is about the men . . .

I am a eunuch. We vote, it is allowed.

THE LAST DAYS

We haven't added to this record in three years. It was thought lost and then remembered, stuffed in a pillow. We searched our thousands of pillows and found it in the last pillow searched, which we expected. Searching for us means that we ordered our eunuchs to search while we, naked, cast grapes into each other's mouths, stoned each other with grapes, says who? Says a high voice, someone who won't take credit. We forgot this record because life is for forgetting, or rather, I think, for giving more thought to what was before us and what will be after.

We'll try to understand what's happened, not to forget, but to raise her, our daughter.

The Temple is uninspiring, our dreams are. Gold we have (Mar). During the dedication feast, at the Tabernacle, we stayed indoors. All three feasts, we're inside.

Solomon loves many forbidden women, foreign, most of us are forbidden: the daughter of Pharaoh, women of the Moabites, Ammonites, Edomites, Sidonians and Hittites.

Solomon's God has forbidden him from us, not us from him. Solomon's God is a jealous God. He's afraid we'll seduce Solomon in other ways, seduce him to our Gods.

We love our Gods and sleep with them too, stone between our thighs to keep us young. To make us young, I say. Solomon loves us and ignores our Gods, ignores his God. Serving his God makes him old and ignoring his God makes him old, unable to triumph.

How does he have time to breathe smoke? With seven hundred wives, or is it a thousand? with princesses, with three hundred of us?

We're a woman of six hundred breasts. Solomon, in a light

mood, calls our breasts *apples*. He's the tree, we have seeds for other trees, we're more powerful.

Some of us who began this record are now dead, and live in dreams, and in afterlives of their own beliefs.

We never fight over Gods. We each have to sleep. Solomon is now old and sleeps little, even less than before, which was hardly any. Each hour of night ages him ten years.

The less able he is to perform, the more attracted to us he becomes, the more attracted to our Gods. He questions us, does not submit. He's no David, apparently.

A eunuch killed a green snake yesterday that had slithered in through a window. He's a hero (we must remember which one he is), tonight we'll discuss his reward.

Our Gods are also the Gods of Solomon's wives, but he prefers his wives as worshippers.

Solomon's temple was more for his own glory. David was bloody, but had faith, or so Sarah insisted, Sarah who's now dead, in childbirth. She was Solomon's favorite, he mourned her for three days. We're not sure who his favorite is now, or if he even knows. Sul thinks it's her and so does everyone else (everyone else tells her).

We're raising Sarah's daughter. We continue the work of the women we call our mothers. Because who remembers their homeland? And those who remember, at least dawn-shaped Jazel, would rather forget.

Many of us were gifts, gifts more powerful than the king or king's son who gifted.

Solomon lusts after Ashtoreth, the goddess of the Sidonians, and after Milcom, the terrible goddess of the

Ammonites . . . no disrespect intended to Zilpa and the others: this is Solomon's judgment.

Solomon has erected a temple for Kemosh, the abomination of Moab, on a hill outside Jerusalem, and one for Molech, another of the Ammonites. He served all his wives, worship in place of his duty as a husband, and his wives, jealous, small-minded women, burn incense and offer sacrifices to their Gods. Scents and sounds, strange, come through the lattice, our windows.

Solomon's God is a jealous God, he must be angry. Zilpa knows something funny, her head on the pillow Nin rubs against, they won't share.

The music sounds even stranger, and for the first time (we remember) some complain of its loudness, harshness, its dissonance. We have a new musician and none of us favor him, or at least none of us have admitted to it.

Solomon has encountered his God twice, as much as he told us, and we sleep with our Gods every night.

Solomon told Skinny Hagar that his God will deprive him of his kingdom. They lay next to each other, did not touch. His God has threatened to give the kingdom to another, a servant. For the sake of Solomon's father, Sarah's dear David, almost a God to her, Solomon's God would take the kingdom not from Solomon, but from Solomon's son. Which one? whose? This is what Solomon told Hagar, and what Hagar repeated to us. We were sober and quiet, the eunuchs have us brought more drink.

There are altogether too many Gods. As many as us. What'll we do with them? What have you done with them?

Solomon told Fat Beth that his God would only deprive him

of part of his kingdom. He'll give one tribe away, which one? What are tribes? We're all sisters and Jerusalem will be spared.

We, says Ruth of the Sword Tongue, have gates.

We've heard rumor of Hadad the Edomite, the king's son in Edom, a rival. Nine of us have slept alongside him, the savage. There's much strangeness. Through our walls we hear rumors of Rezon, the son of Eliadah, prodigy of the king of Zobah. Probably related to Solomon somehow, besides being another rival.

Moons have passed, three bleedings. Blood of David, Aya of Gezer says, old peace, riches of Solomon. We've been too bloody to continue, to understand. Blood, the Gulf of Akabah, which six of us have bathed in.

Our harem, our sisterhood (Hina the Fawn), began when Solomon's reign began, he inherited none of us from David, and so none of us, to Solomon's people, are old, though some of us are old amongst ourselves.

We hear rumors of Jeroboam, the son of Nebat, an Ephraimite of Zereda, Solomon's servant. We've refused him too.

Damascus, Lin Who Sees With Water says, is windy.

Refusing is not a sign of disapproval, neither does it prevent the act from occurring, it's merely a ritual. Worship is only ritual. We're the ones who are worshipped.

It's said that on the day Jeroboam brought two golden calves, one into Bethel, the other into Dan, a hut was built, and that this hut is to be the first of many, of a great civilization. We'll never breathe that air, either.

We're the nexus of all rumors. Our mouths are fragrant,

and so we open them. Your milk-mouth, says Porta to me, your yogurt-mouth. In our dreams, Solomon's God sings to us songs Solomon claimed were his.

Jeroboam is to have ten tribes, one tribe left for David's sake and one for Jerusalem, the heart of the earth. Solomon will lose his kingdom for the sake of his wives. Wives are terrible, Yellow Ina says, despicable things. What will happen to us? We've betrothed history, three hundred daughters, at least, from our ranks, replacing each one of us. Some sons too. Among us, Solomon seeds mostly daughters. Jeroboam will be the next king is the rumor Jeroboam spreads. His lips reach us, they are cracked by the desert.

The seed of David grows within many of us, none the blossom of the Messiah. We vomit and vomit and are sung to sleep.

More and more, the idols going up aren't made in a sex.

Solomon has made an attempt on Jeroboam's life. We knew this days in advance, days before anyone else knew. We knew it even before Solomon himself knew. His God told us.

We pass my joyous daughter around from hand to hand, breast to breast, some of which milk, we sing and we dance. She's a sister of Sarah's daughter. Who will serve them?

Jeroboam has fled to Egypt, to Shishak, and remains there. Things are quiet and no less strange, music too soft to hear, but there, definitely there. These are the last days.

Solomon has reigned for forty years today and there's celebration as quiet as no music. People are restless. Rays of the sun, says Porta, snapped harp strings. We might be the only ones who remember. I am the new elder, am I worthy?

Solomon, today, sleeps with his fathers, will be buried in the city of David his father. Rehoboam, his son, a legitimate son, will reign. He's untested, at least untested by us. Wives are death. Word's now winding through the desert to Jeroboam.

Fear is the beginning of knowledge, Solomon said, but this proverb has the order reversed. Men instruct, women example.

I'm thirty-six years as of this moon, one year for each eunuch, and I need pleasure as I need air. We hold each other. I am a jug, fill me.

Solomon is a rock, cleave him apart. Release the idol in bondage inside the stone. In our language, *cleave* means both to *rend* and to *adhere*. We are water, vessels are for men, the shapes we might discover ourselves in — the long neck, the wide bottom — exist only to attract them.

A world of only men would die and a world of only women would die, but the world of men would destroy itself.

Solomon should've been a eunuch, should've been born a eunuch.

What history have we raised? What idol? It's not our responsibility to destroy them.

THE ACROBATS

My foot is water, says Lucy. My foot is water, Lucy says.

Lucy who never lies. Lucy whose name wasn't Lucy, really isn't Lucy, she's not a Lucy: she wanted it changed on arrival and she changed, right off the airplane, when we first came over — that's what you can do in this country — contracted with the talent agent who'd caught our act in Belgrade. Though his proposition to Lucy was refused (I, ambivalent as I always was), he still signed us. He or his lawyer took care of immigration, the visas, her name. Mine stayed the same.

We were acrobats, the two of us, Lucy and I. Lived and worked together for the circus eight years, eight years touring the same fifty states (a big country which in eight years didn't get any bigger), eight years living in that trailer. Eight years is a respectable stretch of airtime for a team of acrobats who began young. We would have lasted forever, hung there, suspended, groping for each other.

My foot is water, says Lucy. One day outside L., I think. My foot is water, Lucy says. What do I do? We are acrobats and this is unacceptable. Water is the foot. God Above. Where my foot was is water. Says Lucy. Water is where my foot used to be. Lucy says this to me while she's still in bed. Caravan pulls out in an hour. I'm awake, standing, thinking of sex. My penis is also an acrobat (like father, like son) and I want to enter her. God Above. But from under the covers she says, my foot is water and water is my foot. Framed in the doorway. My American was always better than hers. She lies in the trailer, lies in the bed spread open, hair millions, strung out. Only in bed is she without the tight bun. I wanted to small down and fill her, but I laughed. What do I do?

I tumble to her and throw off the covers. Ivory, apple peel pure, breasts hinting (breasts of an acrobatess), hips rounding — someday, I always thought, after retirement: children — strong legs tapering and her left foot, water. I told you so, she said. I so told you. Water ending or beginning at her ankle, a foot of water, water of a foot. I said, try to walk, and she sat up, hung her legs off the bed, stepped down and one foot went squish — she was spilled, uneven.

We canceled the act that night and consulted the doctor. He touched her water and it rose below the knee, cool water on the knee. Perplexed, he didn't know what to do — how could he? Lucy couldn't help rubbing. Water rose over her knee, flowed up. Couldn't walk and she'd lay, her water soaking the sheets without losing its form, free-flowing as a leg there, leg not strong enough to stand on, certainly not strong enough for acrobatics.

I got another partner, selected him from ten applicants scouted out, a small twelve-year-old boy from China, then sub-missive, once kind, a promising acrobat, those people are. But he's no Lucy. His parents are communists but he was not (he hungered for money): still he accepts fate. I'd nurse her and then do the show — second half, after the lions and before the tigers, center ring — and return, sometimes alone, sometimes with my new partner. We'd tell her about the show until she'd fall asleep. I offered her to adopt him. With her rubbing the water rose above her knee, wetness to her sex.

The old days at night after the show in the darkened tent we'd couple from the trapeze, swing into each other, meet, and I'd penetrate her mid-air, we'd writhe, squirm, and she'd moan at our peak to our fall down to the net: upon impact, buttocks bulging through the netting, together we'd orgasm as one old deaf-mute shoveled up the elephant shit. When we landed in the net at the end of an act — this during the show, no sex for the children — the guitarist in the pit orchestra (though it wasn't an orchestra . . . at least they employed live musicians, another act of charity), a fat young man with glasses, would sound this chord, exactly when we hit. I liked it, knew it, knew it by ear, asked him what exactly it was, he said, E7#9, taught me to play it. I knew it from Jimi Hendrix, who used this chord often, open string, then the chord, guitar of six tightropes. First heard it on Radio Free Europe. Chord sounds, opening up, and we flip over the edge. On Sundays, I'd balance his guitar on my nose and he'd clap and drool. Purple Haze, the lights of the show. *Excuse me while I kiss the sky* . . . which Lucy always thought was: *excuse me while I kiss this guy*. I always laughed, never fixed.

The water made me think of the ocean, of the cruise ship we worked on the off-season, winter, departing weekly from M., a few hours south of where the circus broke down every year. In the middle of that water, sky and water, on a ship, in a hall, flying across the audience . . . Insanity: the world is insane, and the ship rocked. We lived small underneath the waterline, no porthole, not sick, hating it, and promising ourselves and each other we'd never come back. But we always did. And then that one time we flew back to Belgrade when Lucy's mother died, her mother who believed in magic, a practicing witch who couldn't save her own life. Up in the air, a stewardess from Belgrade comforted Lucy in American. I drank red wine produced in the region of my birth, poured into a plastic glass from a green bottle, liquid, fermented grapes thrown through the airspace in a metal tube hurtling at ungodly speeds thirty-three-thousand-six-hundred-fifty-two or something like that feet above the earth . . . whose feet? . . . banking left. The world is insane, its people are.

The doctors had to amputate, they did. They cut off the water. Covered by insurance, Lucy on permanent disability (not much), me on my salary and also supporting Lin, though I didn't have to, when he was short. And he was short often — he spent too much on sequined suits (sequins, the mark of the amateur), hot-dogs and sundaes . . . he'd never gain weight, explode the sequins to spinning. Doctors outfitted Lucy with a plastic and steel prosthesis, a leg as pale as hers was from hip to toe. It plugged in snug. She'd never trapeze again but she remastered standing and walking, even a length of a run. She was back, nearly floating, and she caught me with Lin. I'm an idiot. Idiot that I am. Day she went out to visit her friend the horse trainer, forget her name, pay a surprise visit, show off her regained stride. She stood there in the doorway, stared at us, me aroused, silence, in holy fury. Lin, greased, naked, jumped through the open window, ran for a sundae.

Listen: the circus is dying, all circuses are dying, been dying forever. Paying admission is an act of charity. Parents are to be thanked for supporting the marginal, our small welfare kingdom: midgets who never made Hollywood, wood-paneled sedan pederasts, liquor store holdup men who'd evaded the system, unmedicated psychotics who now worship quartz, glue huffers, those who don't even misfit in. I'm not afraid of clowns. Only men who play at being clowns are afraid. But not those with skills, me and Lucy — we were professionals, been professionals since youth, deserved the attention, the money . . . artists, athletes. We were the top of this pile, pile of menthol and tattoos done with heated pen tips, transient dreams, shit and stubble. God Above.

Caught with Lin, aroused, I dropped my head, sorry, truly apologetic, but apologies aren't instant . . . apologies are falls which last forever, no net. Lucy detached her prosthesis, leaned herself against the wall, began to beat me with her prosthesis, heaved it at my neck again and again, disembodied kicks, my head was getting heavier, and heavier, chin to my chest and my head dropping. What was happening? I am quite flexible. My head lowered itself . . . my neck couldn't hold it up . . . it fell slowly . . . Lucy beating harder and harder in silence . . . my head fell to the floor, too heavy to hold up anymore. Not an increase of size but of weight. Couldn't pick it up. Doubled over at the waist, as if praying, my head on the dirty floor. (Lucy never cleaned anymore.) I said on my way down, Lucy, I'm serious, Lucy (though I never called her Lucy) . . . I can't pick my head up on my own. She screamed now, held it in then let it out, dropped her prosthesis and disappeared, or I couldn't see her anymore. The Strong Man, forget his name too, jumped up the steps to our trailer, pulled the door off its hinges, tried to lift my head and failed . . . not happening . . . tried to lift me entire and of course he did, except my head . . . that remained on the floor. They tied three elephants to a rope and the rope to me, around my head, knotted under my nose. Couldn't move me. Grounded, flight grounded. Head was too heavy, all blood rushing to it. My head is heavy and heavy is my head.

Listen: we didn't do arenas, stadiums, no, we're still a touring outfit, something to be proud of understand, town to town. You need to know the legend, the lore. Pick locks of memory with skeleton keys. A woman is popcorn: she needs to be heated and thrown around a bit. Not what I've learned, what I've known. Setting up the tent and pulling it down in the morning. A three-week run in any one place at the most. We discourage most from joining . . . (I should've discouraged you, gone with the Latin girl instead . . .) I should've listened to my own advice, but it was my father who pushed me here, my dead father. Children clapping, imitate, ape. I'm probably responsible, or my act is, for tens if not hundreds of jumps off roofs and triple somersaults turned out windows. But maybe I'm flattering myself. All is vanity. Still, I tell my visitors: Come visit the circus grounds the day after the day, tomorrow: that's what those families are like, empty, empty except ruin. Lucy and I were in perfect health, top form and all that.

Not anymore, with my head on the floor, the floor under my head.

Doctors failed, gave up, quit . . . we needed the old circus men: the snake oil salesmen, the all-purpose tonic hawkers. Now there was nothing to do. Nothing to do except charge marks money to try and lift me, as a sideshow. One dollar a lift. Lift his head and win a grand. A pity I didn't think of this earlier, said the Ringmaster, also the Manager. I could've used you and your wife. Lucy was never my wife. She would say I hesitated and I would say she, same thing. They exhibit me in my trailer, walk marks up the steps, through the new door, pick their pockets as they enter, here, to lift me, to meet me grown old, gray and out of shape, fat. Spine worthless, muscle tone gone. Fat though I eat and I drink and I breathe only the dust, and I'm never hungry, not starving . . . and not an artist anymore, a freak. The floor of my trailer sags under my head, my dead weight. One day while we're driving to the next stop, next town, on the highway, I'll just fall through the floor, floor will give way, fall onto the highway, trailer doing fifty or sixty, Lin driving . . . to be crushed underneath the old wheels. Or is my head stronger than that? When tires meet skull, will my head flip the trailer and the truck pulling? My head hanging now, a distended penis, half-filled and half-empty, wilting in desire, from desire. I shit here and they scoop up my droppings, the elephants' deaf-mute and his shovel. Elephant memory. Lucy's circus friends — she always had more friends than me — come to visit, free of charge, of course, and laugh. At my head, heavy. At my heavy head.

No one has yet lifted me and I make decent money. How could I spend? I give to Lin who betrays me. Last I heard of Lucy was a letter apparently postmarked F. Lin read it to me, said he thought it was stained with tears. Shows what he knows. We get our mail forwarded to wherever we are once every two weeks, and so by now she might be gone. She wrote in American — why?

Dear Lubo,

I'm well here. Bought a small ranch house and a dog I haven't named yet. Don't know why. He licks me all day, eats me. Because now I'm all water, or what's left of me is water, laying here in an inflatable pool by the porch door. Soon I'll be gone. Dictating in waves to my postman who brought the cashed check. He gets ten percent. Disability takes care of everything. Hope you're well and your head's feeling better. Regards to Lin. And just so you know I don't expect a letter in return.

Sincerely (Once Yours),

Lucy

Here I am, voice echoing off the near floor, dictating to Lin, his daily American lesson, without any way to fix mistakes.

THE WALL

If my wall was this testament, there would be no more words. My wall is empty in this empty lot, no graffiti, not here. Outside the urbis, amid the sprawl (where it's too desperate for graffiti), where I am now, the stars above are enough to make me want to pluck out my eyes in some depraved act of Greco-Romance. Inside, in the interior, where I once lived with Janice and Simon, there were no stars — stars disappear there above the main drags, dim out, dim like the people there . . . and everything has the eventual tendency to flatten. Down one of those drags, heading away, running away from whatever it is my wife and my old shrink (and her shrink who knows my shrink, my old shrink, knows him I think more than professionally) away from whatever they say I'm running from, past strips of insurers and usurers and retail outlets, past my old firm's old office, past summers and into the unseasonable openness, through invisible walls, through invisible walls within invisible walls . . . and here I am, here. Eating pickled eggs from a jar the tender doesn't know I have, doesn't know I took, doesn't know I hide between my thighs to keep them warm. Drinking whatever anyone'll pour me. And this is all I have to show for myself, this wall. My whole life, this wall. The justification of my existence whole, this wall, an albatross nest atop . . . if I lose my humor, I lose everything . . . Simon, the name of my dead son, Simon the name of no one here except my past. I've sunk most of my money into this wall. I've spent — my wife, okay ex-wife, would say wasted — ten years of my life on this wall, and so I've earned my rage, my hatred for everything that would be under the moon if there was any moon tonight. I am this wall and this wall is me, and we are both here, for now. Ten years ago next week, Simon, my son, then nine, rode his bicycle into this wall, my wall. His spine snapped on impact, he died. I was a lawyer then, my wife a lawyer too, we were both lawyers. Not knowing why, I purchased this wall, my wall. The wall is freestanding in an empty lot between the Drain, my preferred drinking establishment, and an abandoned factory, a factory which had manufactured umbrellas: everything in and on umbrellas with the exception of the handles, which were made in Southeast Asia somewhere (Vietnam maybe, ask Abel) for less expense than if they were made here . . . they were shipped here and attached on site, *top-quality handles* my friend Marcus says, another regular here at the Drain. And, he says, *I need to get a handle*, hahaha, very funny you goddamned lush. The wall, according to Abel, Abel Greenberg, the man who sold me the wall, was an interior wall in his, Abel's, father's warehouse, a storage facility — it, the wall, was the only thing that survived the fire which ruined Greenberg Sr.'s dreams of a Miami retirement and a maybe tropical death. My wife, my ex-wife, left me after I bought the wall and I started sleeping out here, in the open, where I could see the stars — thought I was going insane, and maybe I am . . . if I am it's fine with me. I obtained a restraining order preventing her from getting within a specific distance, I forget what exactly, of the wall, which obviously prohibits her from leaving asters here in late summer, on the anniversary — as she did the first three years, until she met Richard . . . Janice, how is Richard, by the by? — Richard, Dick, and how is Janice? *Another round, please, on you.* The freshly-woken and showered tender — whom I've never bothered to meet and who's never bothered to meet me, though I know everyone else here and he knows everyone too, all these freaks, whatever knowing means — he keeps tabs in his private mind, and he knows what I owe and it's enough. Feeling — I insist that I never think and Marcus, or is it Kurt, is inclined to agree, *aren't you?* — feeling that I'd have to leave my place of employment to devote my full attentions to the upkeep of the wall, I'd left to this place, my *preferred drinking establishment*, across from the wall, within spitting distance, facing this lot where old umbrellas wind around towards the edge of the factory district . . . so loud, metal spokes on the asphalt, it's impossible to feel here. *And now — get this! — they want to tear it down! Who? The goddamned State, tomorrow — that's who! Tomorrow!* They want the wall, say it's part of *gentrification, prettification, updating* the factory district. Where my son, my only son, died is not an eyesore! You fathom the testicles on these individuals? So you know what I'm going to do? I'm taking this outside — I've got a thermos if someone'll fill it — and I'm going to sleep and wake and eat and shit in front of my wall, all day now, forget this place, refusing to move for these people. *I mean, who the hell do they think they are? Eminent domain* hitting me like a theological term . . . and I don't even believe in God anymore! I've got all my legal books — keeping them warm under me, giving me height on this stool — examining the cases, the precedents, what recourses I have . . . *I have my rights!* Eggs between my thighs, books under my ass. What about my rights? *My Simon had such promise, Marcus.* How much promise you're supposed to ask. *More promise than any one of you schmucks.* He was a wizard, a genuine prodigy, a rare talent and he rode his bicycle, first bicycle without training wheels, a great and bright and clear summer day . . . the kind of day that becomes in your memory every summer day. And my son goes and rides it into a wall and dies. *Talk about not doing anything half-assed! That's a son of mine!* And you want to talk about running up against walls? My appeals: denied. My appeals to those appeals: denied. My request to represent myself (couldn't go with Janice or Richard): denied . . . Jesus, I'm feeling like Jesus here. My ex-wife — anyone got a quarter? a quarter? twenty-five cents, anyone? — here's the pay telephone spiel: *Lenny, give it up*, she says, *It's time to move on — I have.* Have you? *You haven't even been to the cemetery Lenny!* But he's dead there, no answers there — the wall's the responsible party, accountability starts here, here's where things should sort themselves out . . . here's the immovable object. Hello there, Richard, I hear you there smiling. You have another son now and I ask, Janice, *How's Sam?* And she says, I know you've heard this Marcus, she says, *Why should I tell you? Who are you to him?* — well, the answer is that I'm his inadvertent father. But who was I? I was known as a pillar, a *prominent* attorney, a *distinguished member* of many and variegated institutions. I was a *lay member* many times over . . . but lay members don't take things lying down. I worked my way through law school and then supported my wife through her law schooling and then took her into my firm, and then he died and then she left me, and then I left my firm, and then she left my firm, she says our . . . I hired Richard too, right out of his law school, so my money, or money from me, or money I made possible, funded his law school — his first years working paid off his loans and debts. But debts, you want to talk debts? The wall cost me a second mortgage, and then the house (know the judge, get the house) — it's a large wall, not just what you're seeing framed from the doorway of the Drain. *Yes, Kurt, down the drain* — Jesus H. I've surrounded myself with idiots. And then my car, a convertible, and then my savings, the money my father left me, for upkeep. Martino Bros. did a replastering job — lazy sob's nearly tore the thing down — reinforcement work, steel struts, power wash first and then a paint job . . . matching virgin white for virgin white, you'd think it wouldn't take serious . . . *Hello, Marie, looking well, yes, fine, and you?* And the sob's were supposed to *paint around the goddamned stain*! And what do you think they did? They painted over it! I mean Jesus H. mother goddamned, what the hell were they thinking? There was this spot there, the bloodspot, the wall's imperfection or the wall was the imperfection, around the stain — that was where my son hit! — and they paint over it . . . *and the foreman, Martino himself* . . . keep my voice down he's a friend of Paul's . . . the guy says to me: *Sorry friend, but I didn't think you'd want a stain on your wall. I mean why go through all the trouble to redo a wall and leave a stain on it like that? And as long as I'm saying so, what do you want with that wall anyway? I mean: this whole district's over, slated for wreckage. But it's your dollar, friend, your dollar* . . . *You're goddamned right it's my dollar, you schmuck!* And I told him the whole story and he said he was sorry and then — get this! — the guy offers to paint another stain on the wall, *almost exactly* like the one he painted over . . . he said he could do it *from memory*, and then acted offended when I exploded on him.

Can you believe it? What would he stain it with? *My blood? . . . No one's blood, Paul, no one's, wasn't talking to you, no, enjoy.* And they're there tomorrow morning, wrecking crew from the State, unionized demolishers . . . *And yes, one more and that's that — I'll pay from the settlement money, I'm good for it.* Marcus'll walk me out across to my wall, and he'll stay with me — he's a gardener for some rich schmuck, old friend, up the Gold Way, property on the marshes, another redeveloped section. And then I'll wait — I've got a warm quilt here, a thermos, empty . . . and the jar of pickled eggs, some sweetened nutshells left over from . . . and the books, cook them and eat them — but cook them in what? A puddle? *Goodnight, yes. Alright, so wish me good luck . . .* Marcus won't come . . . *I'll pay you tomorrow — you know I'm good for it, and yes though that's what I always say . . . it's true or at least I mean it . . .* He's got some woman keeping him in watered . . . excuses, excuses, excuses, a triple and I'm on the rocks. I'm here, shoot me, seriously — or come stick notes in my cracks . . . yes, it's cracking already — *where's my guarantee? The one I paid hand over fist over hand over fist over hand over fist for? And how many hands is that and how many people are required for* that? Yes, come and pray, one and all, and to any and every nonexistent God, for whatever you like, at my free-standing wall, facing in every direction at once. Come and I'll trade you umbrellas for presence — I've more umbrellas than raindrops tonight, and some are just spokes without fabric stretched and the sounds these make winding across the lot from the Drain to my wall, echoing off my wall, are enough to make me truly, absolutely and under any definition *insane . . .* can't think and don't want to anyway. *So, come on out tomorrow and face them with me! Testify to the wall, to the redemptive powers in its possession.* And you — *come with your court-orders and mandates and uniforms and force, pure force . . . you want force? Force, irresistible force, is that which is most still, is me. Is me, here. I can't hear you Marcus! — you'll have to come over here if you have something to say, and say it, and bring a bottle while you're at it, and some glasses and ice and let's have ourselves* — but he's gone. The Drain's closing up for the night and with its lights out, and the moon which stayed home tonight, the stars are even brighter and clearer and my wall is even whiter and the dark is even darker and I'm alone, here . . . trying to push my wall across the State before morning, across the stateline, the river, before — I'll concede — guaranteed destruction not to mention serious legal problems, fees, hundred eight hours billed per day, debt, prison, rape, death, murder or not, and then what'll I do without any family or job or wife or friends or money or wall? No life. Yes, I'll push my wall across the State, and into the river, where it'll be my raft — it'd float! — and I'd raft down the river until the river spills out into the open ocean . . . the stars should be *breathtaking* out there . . . and from there, who knows? I'll float, maybe . . . maybe right off the edge of this flattening world.

EULOGY FOR A POEM

I am here at the request of the family, you, a family so large and far-flung as to be almost inconceivable, gathered here, today, altogether for the first time in my memory since we buried Peter — and sad it must be for occasions such as these — to bury *him*.

But how well did we truly know him? And what is truth anyway, besides one of his old concerns? That was back when he still had concerns. We knew him as well as he let us. He was notoriously difficult — his was a difficulty which allowed us to discover ourselves in the process of discovering him.

I feel terribly self-conscious speaking here, today, in front of all of you. So many minds here and why me? *He* never asked me — *you* did. Perhaps because he dedicated himself to me. But we all claim an intimate, exclusive relationship with him — don't we?

He lived in us, he lived through us. We were only hosts, witnesses. And his death is also our death, a losing of ourselves. Inexplicably, I'm speaking ex tempore, and also from memory, and it's failing me, now. However (and here's the irony) *our* death is *poetic*, and *his* is *real*. My words will never match his — it's amazing to think that we exist in the same language.

How many dead mouths spoke of him? This funeral, his funeral, reminds me of how many mouths should be here today. How many mouths now reciting earth, how much old breath, should be here today to pay him tribute, mouths more worthy than mine. Peter kissed me once in New York — the first kiss I ever had from a man — and I felt young. But *he* was perpetually young, wasn't he? And he acted so old, ancient — an age and a wisdom which, we must admit, was cultivated, as was his only form: tragedy. Which reminds me of *Death's*, which Jonathan Roth wrote, influenced by him — I hope you don't mind me quoting you, John, they're beautiful lines:

> *Death's*
> > *heart the room of*
> *A sui cide*
> > *ighed anecdotal*
> > > *Will*

We, poets even if we're not, gathered here today to entrust him to the earth, have small hope, also, of understanding his true beginning. Knowledge of the days of silence, of void, of the hardenings, is denied us. The late, silent evenings when he lay there alone, not quite reconciled, not quite at ease with who he was — and now I'm supposed to give my account? He gave me earfuls. How could we even struggle with the idea of cause? His existence was his creation, perpetual, also at Peter's hands, I'd say, and his creation was his existence. So what of origins? I, as many of you, knew Peter well. Peter, his adopted father, his mentor. And even he, Peter, our dead's most intimate acquaintance, wouldn't presume to understand, or explain, his prodigy.

The nearest we can come to the beginning of his lineage is nowhere near enough, just as this grave, here, is not his end, not quite. His beginning, as distant as I understand it, was in Carthage, is in Carthage, wherever Carthage the Celestial is now. His forbearers were men of war, men who lived to the young age at which they were to die. Admittedly, to these men he was the merest glint — he was their fame, their hopeful immortality, and yet he did not occur to them, at least not as he was — his conditions were not yet set.

From Carthage there is no direct descent, but there rarely is. I apologize for this wandering — like many of you, I knew him once by heart, but I will not recite and I ask you not to, either, ask you to respect my wishes . . . he must be *remembered* not *revised*. And I've promised myself to keep this short.

But who could fail to notice his Anglophilia? It is to London, but Rome as London, were he can next be traced. Yes, we have skipped the Classics — he knew them only in translation, and his mentor, Peter, was unable to enlighten him in the originals. Peter, who fled to London the night before the war and there, in a small flat in Middlesex, grew a new name to match his new moustache — remember the moustache? Yes, our dead is not alone in having no true name. And then to the New World, to New York, but New York as the last city in Europe, the last European capital. Peter once said to me, at a poetry fête in Berlin, where he'd been drinking — he had to drink to believe he wasn't in Berlin — he said, *I am the last European* . . . what Brecht or Scholem, I forget, said of Walter Benjamin, he said of himself. But Peter's prodigy, the body we bury today, I insist was not European, nor was he anything else. He was far too displaced for that distinction — *heimatlos*, according to Rilke's formulation . . . though he, and Peter, often doubted Rilke's sincerity.

I first merited his acquaintance even before I met Peter. It was a rainy afternoon in New York, I was having some friends over for dinner and — Talia, do you remember this? You, my dear friend, brought him. And then — forgive me Talia, and you too John, and Edward — it's as if you three disappeared, and it was just me and him, him and me . . . and I let the soufflé burn, didn't I? But this is too precious a memory, too much mine.

Peter's death, that was last time we all got together, wasn't it? His teacher, his beloved and loving mentor, his adopted father I would say, retiring Peter, predeceased him by, what is it? ten years now? Peter's death came even as his language was ailing. He was Peter's justification, when he was discovered, in his mentor's late age. *My greatest*, Peter said to me another night, in Paris. *If anything*, he said, *then this is my immortality —* we'd been drinking . . . Peter was always drinking, especially in Europe. That's what killed him fast: drinking. Europe is what killed him slow. But if deaths have different worths, importances, then his death is the more significant, the more painful . . . for me. Who was the student anyway, him or Peter? And weren't they, finally, one in the same?

He died of Peter dying, he died of his language dying, he died of the ethics, ideas and images he invoked dying, many of which, we must admit, are already lost on us. He spoke of panthers in a milk bar pacing around empty tables. But how much longer will panthers be around? And for what purpose, and for whose purposes, will they be kept? Will tomorrow understand, will it imagine, the panthers' sweet breath, and that as a reference to Aristotle? Or the image of the panther as Jesus, from the book of Hosea, unto Ephraim? Probably not.

And how many milk bars are closing left and right these days? Peter and I used to meet in one in New York, and eat herring after herring — he said to me, *The salt keeps me alive . . .* which is ironic when you remember that he, newly dead he, invoked many times the ancient practice of salting the earth to prevent next spring's harvest . . . another example of his cultivation. So who could hope to understand him in fifty years, besides those of us who are contractually obligated to understand him? Most of us, dear family, will be dead. Will there be a family left to bury us, and if so, what will be their concerns? Now I know only my love for him — love he defined for me.

Your last words to me, dear friend with no name, your last words to the world, nameless friend, let them be the last words spoken over you, words I will remember here:

> *While ash*
> > *loose s*
> *I'll*

Six Dreams

I am the man they killed and unspooled his intestines which they strung between him and a bent lamppost across town. This is the tightrope I am walking, this intestine, and strangely, and anonymously, the man they killed, slumped on a rooftop, is me.

Important that this information's recipient not be shaky on the preceding point: the man whose intestines are strung between himself (myself) and a bent lamppost, and the man who is now walking these intestines, is the same man, is me.

This is the line, below me, which carries their information. Information along the lines of: statistics and interpretations of price fluctuations in gasoline, market predictions for the red-onion trade, famous women's lingerie measurements, and so on. And so, as information is transmitted, the line vibrates, which makes my life that much harder, staying upright, not falling. I can feel this information, my feet have learned to interpret its movements, to read them. Weighty, philosophical information, as well as joking, produces negligible vibration — it's with the trifling and gossip that I wish I possessed the power of flight. My feet are my sole sources of information, or at least the only sources I trust. I have two feet, the Talmud requires two witnesses.

Walking away from myself, I have never reached the lamppost, probably never will. If I did, I like to think I'd just turn around and head back, to myself. My sources, their information, tell me that the lamppost used to light the sidewalk outside a physician's office, a pediatrician. Used to light because I've learned that the bulb went out, and was never replaced . . . that's why it's so dark. The physician must practice in darkness. His upstairs neighbor, his fat daughter, living in an apartment he rents for her, hangs her underwear out on the line — and so as the information is transmitted, it sometimes becomes wet. There is nothing more dangerous to me than wet information. One day I'll slip, and fall away from myself . . . and then what?

Possibly I am seeking his treatment, the physician's. Possibly that is my purpose. We are in pain. Always in pain. This is worse, far worse, far more painful than being a human bridge, though I do not derive this opinion from personal experience. I am on the other end of this line, gut ripped open, sitting in a hard-backed chair atop the roof of a laundromat. Laundromat which always shakes and sometimes jumps from the perpetual activity of the machines inside. His fat daughter could do her wash here, but she doesn't. She washes her oversized shrouds in her bathtub, hangs them out to dry on my line, clothespins pinching the information, impeding the flow. My self sits there, and I am projected here. I am information not strung, just particles thrown forward and assembled on the most tenuous of grounds. Whenever I step, it hurts me, causes me indescribable pain, wrenches me forward, slumps me in my chair. But I do not fall down, off the roof, will never, I cannot. I am seeking treatment.

Posture should concern everyone, not just young women, the fat daughter. I stand here as if a spoke from a wheelchair's wheel was grafted to my spine. For additional balance, I clutch a length of air, which isn't much, sometimes thick, sometimes thin, depending on the fire situation below. Often the burning, always *controlled* (or so the information assures me), is intense. Smoke rises, dark, and that's why I can't trust my ears and eyes and nose. I'm sure the undersides of my feet are incredibly blistered and calloused. I don't know what they're burning below me — that's not included in the information. Possibly they're entertaining the thought of burning the information itself — my line has sometimes been threatened. But I'm not worried. They need the line as much as I do. It's just that they're tempted, amusing themselves, asking themselves maybe: *What can we do without?*

I sometimes think of my mother, remember. It has to do with the umbilical cord. But I'm not fed information. Instead, their information seems to be my waste product, the product of a natural process for which I'm not obliged to apologize. Where is my umbilical cord now, my now ashen and shrunken lifeline? My mother lived her entire life without asking a single question. Thoughts of my mother do not constitute information. It's occurred to me that no one might want to know about my mother. This assumption seems fair, and I doubt my mother would've disagreed or been offended by it. If she were alive, she'd assume I am responsible for my present condition.

I sometimes think that the lamppost, the physician, his fat daughter, that all of it is an imagining, that my feet crossed themselves and my toes, in fear, gripped onto the wrong set of coursing information, confused. This thought is more a fear, however I'm willing, and unafraid, to exist within any interpretation. It's quite possible that my innards, this line, stretches out forever, tied to nothing at all at the other end, just stretching out, whether infinitely or not. Maybe my intestines just end and hang straight, suspended there, beyond smoke, in space.

Possibly there are others who share my predicament, whose intestines run parallel to mine. (They must run parallel, they must avoid intersection, mix-ups: all information must flow in one direction. Not that any one direction is correct, just that one direction must obtain to realize any progress.) And so, contrary to Euclid and his disciple Spinoza, it pleases me to imagine that somewhere our parallel intestines, impossibly, meet and run into one. And that we are all perpetually walking our lengths of intestines to that far-off impossible point, a star hiding itself just now in smoke and daylight. That is the irreducible point — the point shining over a river starred with rocks which once formed a low stone bridge — where all information gathers.

But we have decided to discard the perpetual. All of us sitting in hard-backed chairs atop buildings, our intestines stringing out, will walk on our intestines, will run, leap, until our intestines meet and intertwine. Then we'll all follow each other on our common length, in single file, to the distant star. (It's my sincere hope that our combined weight doesn't pull the star down out of the sky, fall it down to earth.) And there we'll all live, free from our attachments, our bodies, free to discuss and form ideas. (One idea: disembowelment is the foremost enabler of individual freedom we have thus far evolved, however accidental that evolution.) Upon reaching our destination, our goal, we'll know all, least important of which the identity of our common murderer. And then we won't reel ourselves in from those terrestrial rooftops, no. Instead, we'll sever our ties on the sharp edges of other stars

and watch our cords fall to earth, getting heavier with the long
fall, gravity-pulled, crushing all, raising dust.

We have some explanation due.

I wake up alone to the sound of the workmen and stagger out of my room, groggy, awake with a headache. I go into the next room, the room I usually avoid, the room she's taken over, to say my one daily word to the girl: *Hello.*

The girl sits in the middle of the next room, sitting atop a low, small white object, straddling it, just waiting for me. The object is a white square, a cube, its weight to be determined by the person who is to lift and throw it, by me. A cube to be launched into flight soon, into space, by me.

How heavy, or light, should I will it?

I bend over and decide the cube should be light. Having made this decision, it's still a serious effort to carry the cube outside, and I'm soon sweating. All the construction workers are lined up in two silent rows down the street, lined up on both sides on the sidewalk, all the workmen who've been tearing up the street, who for the past ten months have dug holes and filled holes and dug holes again and again in front of my house. The workmen who've been drinking cheap beer and smoking cigarettes so poorly rolled they nearly fall apart every time they're lit. I've hated their trash outside all these months, their discarded cans and bottles, their butts and packs. Holding the cube is becoming a difficult proposition. I begin to think the cube is a chunk of street they've dug up. If I it is, how did the girl get it? My arms feel alternately weak and stiff.

Finally, the girl nods at me, smiles, and I run a few steps, down the street, hoping to add some momentum to my throw. I release the cube from two hands, workmen on both sides of me forever, almost throwing from my groin, and the cube goes up in the air . . . not too high, but it seems to disappear . . . no one sees what happens to it, no one knows. The workmen soon lose interest, mull about, smoke and grind ash on their shoes and the sidewalk, gossip and laugh, point with their hands of all thumbs.

I head inside, alone.

A pure, bonewhite chessboard and all the pieces, both white and black, have rubber-stamp undersides. The ink is inexhaustible. Each piece, each regular-sized piece, somehow, stamps the shape of its move on the chessboard, ink perfectly filling in the traveled squares. I constantly pick the pieces up over my head, wondering how it's possible, but each seems regular. Though I'm only playing black, and I have no opponent, the chessboard is a mess of ink, black, pitch, a hole I jump through, for no obvious reason, a hole I fall through, down a hill, swerving my way around faceless couples, disposed without evident logic, loving and sleeping on mattresses half-buried in the sand of the slope. I slide down, down into a hallway, sandgrains on linoleum flooring, an overlit hallway stuffed into a stocking, the hallway maybe a hollow leg, a leg of hallway which bends, at the knee, sending me tumbling further, tumbling inside a thumb toe, where I stop, gather myself warm under the nail, and sleep.

A tower with water pooled on top, water neck-high, neck-deep, atop the tower and yet the water is contained by no wall, only floating still, floating immovably on the roof of this tower. A tower, then, with water pooled neck-high, neck-tall, atop.

Slabs of wood, doors maybe, some rectangles, without handles, some odd and hooked, float on the surface, atop the water, atop the tower.

I stand, naked and greased, on a slab, wobbly, legs spread, ass out for balance, and then, tired after awhile in the sun — which is immediately overhead, as if I could touch it — and overbitten by gnats, greenheads and mosquitoes, I lie down on the slab, on my stomach, and now either sleep or am pulled out to the edge. And despite my efforts, I can't help myself from going over the edge. No water falls off the tower, not drop one — the water remains still — and the slab falls or doesn't fall, but I fall, many stories. It's a residential tower, but where are the residents?

I fall many stories, hitting the rocks at the tower's base — the slab does not hit bottom — and I am not hurt, or it doesn't hurt. I prop myself up on my elbows, examine my stomach and find a wound like a target, many circles circumscribing each other. And then I roll off the rocks to the thin beach, and from the beach I roll into the marshes and then into water, rolling dazed, gluttonously. The tower is on an island, almost takes up the entire island.

In the water, I don't struggle, just calmly go under, and a child sees me and alerts his father, a fisherman, and they, in a small motorboat, save me, and someone I know, at least some-one who seems very familiar to me, hands me a towel on the other shore, shore lined with fir and pine trees, alternating, planted equidistantly along the circumference. The tower was on an island, its base ringed with rocks and then a thin beach and a thin ring of marsh, and then a circular lagoon, light water, and a circular further shore and who knows how many other rings within rings? Maybe marsh again, then beach, rocks, another tower, water, another me . . . and then this identical infinity repeated, nested atop *my* tower . . . and the others . . .

Someone I know but cannot identify doesn't thank my rescuers, and drives me home.

A house of book, a bookhouse, a house containing a book and a book only, no room for anything else, a book the size and floor-plan of a house, covers and pages filling and accommodating the space and layout. There are pages of floors and pages of ceiling and pages, bottom-cover the floor and top-cover the ceiling, pages bulging out the windows, pages even stepping up the stairs. The book is always shut, as are the house's doors, must be shut, would burst the house if opened, must never be opened.

Wondering what is written, I stand outside.

I was standing at the end, the dead-end of a narrow hallway, facing the dead-end wall of this narrow hallway. I was standing a breath from the plaster wall, thin, more of a membrane than a wall, semi-quasi-translucent, but white, white plaster.

But I was there, am here still, or some of me, and why? I can't listen, must forget to listen, even as tired as I am from all this travel. Why did I return? why? A screen kept giving me these obscure messages: an enormously fat descendant of slaves swallowing linen handkerchief after linen handkerchief, an underfed psychic rapping tabletops and selling sperm, his, in autographed vials, between summonses, a spray that will remove your eyebrows to another, previously inaccessible, dimension . . . But my neck hurt in my awkward (and necessary) disposition of eye and ear.

I'd come to this hospital because T., an acquaintance of ours, of mine and S.'s, had shouldered me at the fish store and told me that S. was in the hospital, this hospital, recuperating from the after-effects of major surgery. He wasn't going to die — he was recuperating — but he wasn't well, and, you know, his family's far away, doesn't exactly get along well with his father, you understand, all of this years ago, and on and on. Crux of it was that I should visit S., and T. had already done so, that afternoon, and then had stopped at the fish store, to pick up a few fillets of salmon to serve to a girl he'd met last week in a park.

I nodded, listened to him as I watched a clerk weigh the pink flesh, gray underneath and at the edges, and wrap it in green paper. I once derived enjoyment from the fish store, enjoyed touching the shaved ice, the gathered glaze of dead eyes, the morning after smell.

Now all of those impressions, which I didn't remember having, seemed false.

Memory sensed slavery, memory the method of control.

Because I was the only person, I suppose, in this enormous metropolis to have been embarrassed out of the language, out of my language. I arrived home, that home, the old home, only three nights ago, from abroad — where? And my first visit, after I was humiliated at my parents' house, was to the fish store, and now, here, the hospital. I suspect that maybe it's not mine anymore, this language. I heard it, even spoke it, it might have been the only language I knew. But I was too embarrassed to claim it, had begun to doubt its utility. I have relinquished responsibility for my language, now.

I was walking to the hospital, three balloons I'd just purchased at the party store, three balloons inflated with helium and tied around my left wrist: yellow, yellow, and a red.

These balloons were, as the salesperson at the party store said, *Scented, lemon and raspberry, and they taste like it too. Lick them and they'll dissolve in your mouth — here, try it . . .*

I declined, paid, thanked her wordlessly and left, walking the ten long avenue blocks to the hospital. I felt ridiculous walking with three balloons tied around my wrist, two different yellows, as one yellow balloon was significantly more inflated than the other. But, I suppose, one lemon prevailed.

At the receptionist's desk, I waited five minutes for visiting hours to begin. One minute past the hour, I asked for S. and was told he wasn't on file, to try the emergency room, see if he was there and if he could see me, was in proper shape. *Presentable* was the word the receptionist used. I went, followed instructions. Searching for the ER, I must have lost myself and ended up here, at the end of a hallway leading to nowhere, up against the thin wall, the membrane.

One of my three balloons, the raspberry red one, popped on an exposed lightbulb directly above my head. Startled (I didn't awake), I was now in darkness, a darkness required for me to notice the television set above me, wall-mounted, on mute, now the only source of illumination: a folk-singing evangelist born without middle fingers, a monkey with giant gums, healthy, which spelled the word *monkey* out on the screen, more accurately on the lens of the unfortunate who was filming, spelled it out in pastel:

first MONEY,
then NOMEKEY,
then KONE MY (an animated banana peeled itself and
frowned to the uppermost right of the screen)
and then again MONEY.

My hallway dead-ended somewhere in the middle of another hallway, a hallway running perpendicular to the hallway I was dead-ended in. If there hadn't been my thin wall there, the two hallways would've intersected. My hallway, its outer wall jutting into the other hallway, it seemed, was, suppose, an afterthought on someone's part — whose? And what didn't they want me to find? the insects scissoring their long legs down the forbidden hallway, outlines barely visible through my wall, beetle-clicking to each other? But no, there are words I understood, my ear pressed against the giving plaster.

> Who was your best kiss? or if not best, then most memorable? Giggling. Definitely not –interpolate a foreign name here– in –interpolate an exotic location here, a metropolis without vowels–. Doors opening and shutting. You mascara-wearing music-teacher! Who's the terminal? High heels or is it insect walking down a linoleum floor. So's it's more towards the. It's not worth it, no, never is. I'm sick of you, Jessie. I've spent so much with you. Pay up front, please, yes, up front.

This is where I was and what I was doing, listening, watching, shuddered. And I felt these inner shakings, thoughts of when would I finally understand, be able to assert a pattern, and then leave it, sealed . . . The membrane thinned, the plaster fell into itself.

My body disconnected from my head, head from body, faulty wiring. My head floated up, detached itself, spine came up too, head hovering, spine dangling. I am light, irresponsible for these animals. My body sucked into a vacuum underneath my floating white head, body heaped on the linoleum against the thin wall, under the pulsing television, two shriveled balloons waving from the mess, and a loose string.

Head with the spine attached floated to the ceiling and my head passed through, unscathed. I didn't even tense myself for impact. My spine, unable for whatever reasons to make the passage, hit the ceiling and clattered to the floor, on top of my body.

My spine merged with the loose string, fusing into one length.

My head came up, through the hospital floors, passing through the rooms, through the room of a convalescing rabbi, unnoticed through a kidney transplant operation for a man named Adam (or maybe that's just what the doctor's were calling him), through an overheated room of three pregnant children. I am my head, and so I see and taste and smell and hear, sense.

Floating up towards the roof, feeling the fast air past my ears, head large and white above the metropolis, a metropolis of all outskirts, just outskirts, only streets dead-ending . . . I sensed no accessible middle. My head ascended, past the tall buildings of last century, past the tall buildings now, the enormous office towers and their satellites. Would my head pop on an antenna or spire? No, I gained height, or at this point there is no height, only space beyond the wisps, gained until my head floated alongside the earth, and all the other disembodied ideas in our small universe . . . until I settled, head fixed and set to spin around and around.

Here I am, then, an uninterested party, only an existence, a light's impediment. Until someone, some day, an older man in my imagination, gazing late at night through the crested dawn from the outskirts of the outskirts, frightened, tired, yearning, will, even though I'm small among the small, acknowledge me. Please don't, old fisherman, don't attempt to *wonder* . . . don't begrudge me my chance disappearance, don't begrudge me my failing modesty . . . in this *space*.

If you do spot me, sir, then forget, forget, forget . . . Row home, and to sleep.

Cadenza for the Schneidermann
Violin Concerto

CADENZA, Italian, from the Old Italian *cadence*, meaning much the same as it does in this language, a musical term (excluding the military definitions), a noun. A solo passage intended to feature a performer's virtuosity. A parenthetic pyrotechnic flourish, an ametric tangential, a brilliantissimo *flight of fancy*. Nothing to do whatsoever with living room furniture or the heroine of Monteverdi's *Frottola*. Now understood as a section of a concerto, usually situated towards the end of a first movement, a section reserved for the soloist only, the orchestra having stopped, leaving the soloist to display his instrumental proficiency. Then the CADENZA ends, soloist often signaling his finish with a long trill, and the orchestra re-enters to finish the movement. Though originally a CADENZA was a vocal embellishment, a practice which later extended itself into instrumental music. In opera, a CADENZA was improvised by a performer on a cadence in an aria. Performance practice allowed three CADENZAs in an aria, or *melismas* (as they are known vocally), the third being the most elaborate. What initially interested me about the CADENZA was that it was defined to me, by my friend the pianist Alexander Wald, to whom I dedicate *Schneidermann*, as "an extended solo passage in an *improvisatory style*," italics mine. Meaning that the CADENZA was improvised, ex tempore, up until the advent of Romanticism (and the advent of the famous virtuoso personality), during and after which composers wrote them out, in an *improvisatory style*, a style which derived many of its parameters from instrumental technique. Meaning that the CADENZA focused more on instrumental showmanship and less on a soloist's exploration of a work's thematic material. Third parties — the famous virtuosos themselves — also wrote their own CADENZAs, many written as specialized practice material, and a handful of these became so widely played, and loved, that they, today, seem like they were written into the original score: a prominent example being Joseph Joachim's CADENZA for

Brahms' *Violin Concerto*, overthrown later, to my ear, by Heifetz's. Today, almost no virtuosos perform the CADENZAs of Beethoven or Mozart — which themselves had their genesis in improvisation, in the great tradition of the composer/performer — instead preferring CADENZAs written by mere virtuosi: examples in the piano repertoire are those by Busoni and Reinecke. Today, outside of *modern* or *serious* aleatory musics (which are as deaf to the world as the world is to them), and excluding analogies in *popular*, *ethnic* or *world* musics, almost no virtuosos improvise their own CADENZAs.

— **MUSIC** —

Has the orchestra stopped? desisted?

Everyone finished?

Gasp — it's okay. Air on whose G string?

It's about time I've been wasting until, wasted on this fermata . . .

. . . this bird's eye, staring everything, still. But its shell, in here, this gilt expanse, I've been heating and stirring in and now peck, peck, peck, chickenscratch the orchestra would say (but they're underpaid and overworked, or reverse that): in the man's own handwriting, though I helped some . . .

So, distinguished members and memberesses of the Philharmonic Orchestra, draw out the long bows: downbow for the first violins, upbow for the seconds — the bowings are as necessary as they are Schneidermann's, written into your parts, yes, believe it or not, in his own hand, and such hands! (though I helped some) — and, yes, the final cadence drawn out to the last and stiffest hair, to the frog and to the tip of the bow . . .

Okay, gasp, don't asphyxiate on my cue . . .

Sorry, I'm shouting to be heard over this (Clausewitz's first principle, that of surprise, you know) and then . . .

Okay, a War word, and let's let the resonance die in the nosebleeds, fine.

Listen: I am standing here on stage, under the proscenium arch, in the world's most famous and honored concert hall, in front of the world's most famous and honored orchestra, having finished performing for you the first movement of the Schneidermann *Violin Concerto*. And addressing you instead of performing my solo. Understand. Or this is my solo.

Understand?

Understand? But in matters of art, you decide . . .

    . . . and while you're deciding, allow me to wipe the sweat from my bow and my brow with a handkerchief I pocketed from my hotel, uptown, from the maid's pushtray in the hallway, hotel name of Grand something, you should look it up sometime, everything's marble, and the maid she's some halfbreed, indigene ingénue with the sweetest two loaves, ready for sanctification, tucked away under that off-pink uniform, her name's Maria or at least that's what her nametag has it as, mother of one, twice-divorced and I'll know more tomorrow morning, I hope, or I won't know anything more, I hope, but I'd have filled her F-holes anywhichway, for ever and ever: ewig, ewig as Mahler would have it but only if Schlesinger's conducting, and he's not, I am, sort of, me: the world's representation, and now I am yours. But who am I? Famous enough — my name's ten feet tall but I'm no one, really. Don't be shocked! — the cultured are so easily shocked — don't whisper to each other, don't whisper through the hairs of ears, snort through nose hairs. Because yes, the answer is yes, I have a speaking part, not quite notated, not quite in the program you've read and riffled through the pianissimos and are now flipping through to see if I have a history of mental instability, some schizoid personality disorder that would serve to explain this away. My decision to address you with my voice instead of with my violin. But not quite. I'm relatively sound, ask any of my doctors, all ten of them, who have received complimentary tickets for this evening. And don't see, listen. Not that Schneidermann didn't forehear this, didn't expect this. And, anyway, he's left no explicit instructions as to my address being

unwanted

unwanted, as to my address, this, being unnecessary. Allow me to remind you that it is I, the soloist, the world's famously renowned virtuoso, an essential worker in a non-essential discipline, and now I am yours, fully, truly, away from my instrument, my music, and so forced to descend into life, into the world. So what? Those who praise me, and there are many — though less and less of some and more and more of others with each passing season — praise me as less a violinist than a virtuoso, and less a virtuoso than a musician, a *pure* musician (shades of Pythagoras and O yes, shades, Orpheus . . .) but of what use am I now? All dried up as I am, forsaken by those even unworthy of forsaking me, left for old by Schneidermann and, anyway, who knows from music anymore? Look up *music* in a dictionary, Jesus, and you won't find a picture of me, and Schneidermann's not in the *Grove*, you understand? Yes, might I take a moment of your evening and of my solo to recall Schneidermann? an artistic decision that might allow his ghost, if ghost he is, to rest easier with this liberty I'm taking. Sure, shout out at me like I can hear you, me, just another voice in the din, this heteroglossolalia verging on ipsissima verba in here so that I can for the life of me remember this great man's friendship? kinship? the ship we took over? See this violin you've been tuned to? Owned by Hitler. You hear it? No, it wasn't, but for a moment you believed me and something was different. Schneidermann himself though played this violin (not too well), Schneidermann the refugee, Schneidermann who maybe died insane as you all (should) know the story, maybe read of his disappearance in the newspaper of record or in the glossed magazines that printed-up his posthumous fame, died

insane

insane, maybe, died how though? died anyway or at least I buried him. Schneidermann who gifted me this violin when I'd helped him flee Hitler, so Hitler, in the poetic sense, might have owned it had Schneidermann not been lucky and smart in that order. Sure, nod and grumble like you know from suffering, but none of you are even fit to lick my rosin, and you, from among the orchestra ingathered, one hundred and seven people, one hundred and eight for the second and final movement (if ever we get to it), when the harpist punches in — she's just sitting there lovely now as all harpists, manicured hands folded in lap and mortified — from among you, how many understand what you're playing, really, truly, I ask rhetorically? (Everything the soloist does is rhetoric, don't you know?) In fact, or as my lawyer says, *in point of fact* (which I've never quite figured out), everything nowadays is rhetoric, not rhetoric in the sense of one of the fine arts, as Plato maybe would have it, as an essential instrument, as a staple of every fine not to say total education, and even the boos and heckles and jeers some of you are giving out now are meant to sound without first listening, as if to prove your existence, as if my addressing you doesn't prove it already, so just go ahead! feel free! — people are so afraid to disagree nowadays, to be impolite, and so maybe there is some merit to your grunted responsa. Someone might as well go around to a bodega near hear and pick up some overripe Joisey tomatoes from José or Manuel whatever his name, O Maria — soon enough! — are you here? did you get those tickets? Besides her though, how many of you out there know what you're hearing? She has an excuse, remember, being within a minority meaning a majority nowadays. Yes, sure, hiss, go

ahead

ahead, feel free — sounds like a bad Bratislavian spiccatto, I tell you. Because you don't know what to think if no one tells you, right? Who'll vet your opinion? Let's elect someone then (because democracies are great, except in art), and then have him appoint someone to get those rotten tomatoes. Because misunderstanding, un-understanding, is okay, is fine, is permissible. Even I, myself, well-trained from eight years, had no idea what to think the first time Schneidermann played this, not this, for me in the piano reduction, first day of harmony instruction — a strange discipline, the study of harmony. And he explained it, this piece we've paused in, thusly, as he paced the room, and he paced like an inept attempt at tuning a string (the E-string's fine-tuner, say): tight vibrations and then gradually loosening, slackening right and left, loosing pitch, becoming not music but gut, and gut luck explaining that to Helmholtz. Who's dead, Helmholtz is, as is Schlesinger, who died however as Bruno Walter, and maybe even Schneidermann too, and me soon enough. And gut, cat gut, is what they used to make strings from if you didn't know or forgot — that's what cats are for, ask my friend Katz, he owns ten street versions of them, and then of course the initial stages of violin domestication are often likened unto a cat's screeching, and what hack composer was it anyway who transcribed his kitten tripping across the piano keys and had himself a fugue subject? And who lining a birdcage (Frau Haydn?) or a litterbox with scores of whom (Haydn, Herr Baryton?)? I've never owned animals myself for the simple reason that they are dumb, dumber even than people, than you, believe it or not, but Schneidermann he kept spiders in a jar (as Spinoza, an intellectual pretension),

spiders

spiders he'd pit against each other in death duels, it was not my pets but Schneidermann though (though I am, in a sense, also Schneidermann's pet), and I was to explain this piece to you, but of course Schneidermann was not at all an explained man, not at all, nothing programmatic about him: man and work and work and man, man or work, work or man, same thing or just the terror of popular inquisition (but does that live beyond the grave?), and don't send in your responses, don't care what you think. Anyway, at this remove, both geographic and historical, it's all at best a mystery wrapped in an enigma strangled by a question mark as stooped as his posture. *Enigma*, the word, so used, slips into its own definition, but the word in my own language, my first language, word I learned in shortpants: *rätsel*, near anagram on my own name, surname of Lästerer, meaning of *mocker*, now Laster, a *vice*, and americanized without an umlaut — immigration, my management and my promoters to thank for that. Prefixed by *Gottes* —, as in *Gotteslästerer*, and I mean *blasphemer*, *God-mocker*, and, living up to my name, I mock through my music, and, as a Laster, I last all night, just ask Maria tomorrow, and I've been mocking you all night, now, and you've been paying through your hooked blackheaded schnozzollas for the goddamned privilege of it all, you schmucks, and, what's this? some of you are leaving? already? Why, we haven't even begun yet! — I need to explain. So don't leave, don't leave, don't leave: this thing has a bang-up finale, a real crowd-pleaser. And now not you, you goddamned communist — you all fathom this? My concertmaster's exiting stage right. You can't trust an Asian, can you? they're all so what, so diabolical, inscrutable, and so placid! — well alright

Wang-Lee

Wang-Lee, suit yourself you hack, you have no tone, you have no touch, no feel, you'll never work in this town again, which is all wet with the winter we've been having lately. Because I teach all those people, those Asians — they think they can play but they can't. Maths and music, O the Asians. But if I would've been born an Asian, life would've been that much simpler. You rote monkeys, you deserved Einstein's bomb — I mean, what do you know from ecstasy? what do you believe in? I myself believe in death. That's because I'm supposed to do something with my life, because I have greatness's birthright. Charge of representing the world. Chosen people blah blah blah. And all I need to do now is die, but not yet — still have bills to pay, so I need to do it, this, need to keep this medicine show on the road, traveling, this piece and maybe a few accompanying, don't you know I'm Schneidermann's performing monkey? that I need to keep it going, perpetual motion machine on the eternal return tour, the eternal tour to infinite nowhere? And why? Well, because just like you I've got debts to pay, children to support, alimony and all my money, wives to pay, first wife's children, second wife's children, third wife's children, but calando, calando, calando — an anagram on Doc Alan, my first-call personal physician, my prostate-feeler, hands of an artist which should be cast in bronze or plaster take your pick except for that gorgeous watch of his his wife got him for his fiftieth birthday so he can tell me my time is up, but tell me instead, Doc, are you disappointed I've given up my famous cadenza in favor of this improvised piece of what the mothers, my ex-wives out there, would call dreck, kaka, poop? Come on, Doc, come prima, come sopra, you can answer me — this infamous

soon

soon to be nonpiece of worthlessness in this infamous soon to be condemned hall (one can only hope)? this most famous concert hall named after a man who'd exploited even himself on the way to the top, this hall once built on the backs of immigrant Atlases, steelworkers and railroadmen and now being held up and kept in operation with grants and bequests, digging money out of the grave, how soon until it's shut down? condemned? boarded-up? like CBS' famous 30th Street recording studios (you played here and you recorded there), the old temple, the non-denominational church of all the great virtuosos including yours truly there for his first recordings of the Mozart *Concerti* in 1955, same year as Gould's first recording there, but the studio sold in 1981 to the multinational whim after the last official recording session, and what was it? it was Glenn Gould again, Glenn Gould unavoidable, Glenn Gould doing BMV 988, that's Bach's *Goldberg Variations*, his second recording of it after the famous 1955 sessions in the same space, and the last recording ever in that house before it died into the future: a nightclub or whatever it is now (I never walk by it because I never walk), but that's okay because Glenn Gould escaped back into hiding, back to Toronto, and he never had the same problems I did because Glenn Gould never married, and I did, there was never a Misses Gould and yet there are probably a hundred million Misses Lasters (go ask my lawyers), and they're probably all out here tonight, gossiping, comparing settlements, breastfeeding each other, an entire audience of former and one present but not for long Misses Lasters, Jesus, doing anything besides listening, they never listened, ever. Because whenever I play this original sin Apple

at

at least all of them are in attendance and some of my, how do you say it now? some of my ladyfriends — stand up dears, or not, but at least do me the honor of listening to me, I have something to say to you, to all of you, but first someone get me some water, without gas, Jews hate gas, someone speak to someone more important or go hit a rock or something, descend to the Styx with a commemorative cup. Okay, dears, so which one of you played Euridyce to my Orpheus? Which one of you did I most rescue or did I do the utmost to rescue? From poverty, from misery, from lack of U.S. citizenship, from lack of talent? Who was my Euridyce? Or your-Id-is-she, and don't you out there, you undistinguished mass, pity my violin-shaped women. No one beautiful and rich should be pitied, and you don't believe me? So let's have the house lights, then, please? No? Maybe? So I can see who's leaving through the doors I hear slamming. And here, there goes half the brass section behind me. Definition of *optimism*: a tuba player with a business card. Because friends are as nonexistent as God. Because marital bliss is as nonexistent as God. Or because they all exist only inso-much as God exists, go empty your spit valves on the peaceful faces of your sleeping lovers at home. And, Jesus, the oboists gone too! the tuning Sirens, the touched heads of the orchestra: all that air backed-up, traffic jammed, gives them eventual inevitable enviable brain lesions, didn't you know that? Those lesionaires. Suspect my wife, which one, of playing the oboe — those lips and that absolutely perfect stupidity, the absolutely perfect stupidity of all of them: of my first wife who'd loved me for my music, my second for my fame, my third for my money: divorce, divorce, divorce and now I'm on my fourth, no fifth,

or

or is it? not legally, actually, well, out of the country, fourth I'm
only separated from, or, maybe, ask my lawyer, or my lawyer's
lawyer, he's out there somewhere, or my shrink. But what does
she want me for, number five? Or my shrink's shrink. O let's
say all the reasons previous. She's a soprano — aren't you dear?
and what's the difference between a Lamborghini and a
soprano? Most musicians have never been inside a Lamborghini,
hahahaha . . . but don't let my cough worry you, it's had me for
years. Yes, Doc, I know I should stop smoking, but anyone got a
light? No? O, thanks for the help — a hearty round of applause
for the man in the front row with a book of matches from the
bistro around the corner, *Giorgione's*, a three-star good good
good place, anyone want the phone number? What did you
have? Great. Everyone, he — what's your name? — everyone,
Alvin Feingold heartily recommends the salmon tortellini,
everyone, thank Mister Feingold, great, you have something in
your teeth, just kidding, no one'll notice. Just like no one'll
notice that I have executed, with one minor mistake in my
between me and you absurd second entrance — the bow does
not break like that — I have executed thus far without a conductor. Yes, ladies and gentlemen, heathens and Philistines of
all ages, one tuxedo has held together the first half entire.
Tonight, your eminent musical director, your foreign Maestro
Laureate (because all geniuses are foreign), he's in his penthouse, one of his four penthouses to be less precise, engaging
in anal and oral sex with underaged males, members, yes,
members of your youth chorus and your regular Guest
Conductor — this I have on good authority — a janitor in the
wings, name of Holden, tells me, and janitors, no irony or

slumming

slumming, know everything. Schneidermann, well, not that he wouldn't have indulged, and it's acceptable, permissible to laugh now (warm-heartedly), and it's okay to feel joy, because all homosexuals are essentially optimists and you can understand the reverse of that lemma, and lemma tell you that those who swing pendulum to any pits, half-filling and half-emptying are essentially the only sane ones out there. But at least answer for me this question: why are homosexuals never poor? Always well-groomed and dressed, and don't give me the feminine answer much like the House Manager waving his hands on the Loggia as if he's the Pope or on train departing, pulling out now for the nineteenth century — what do you want? you're doing what? I can't hear you nearly as well as I can hear myself. You know, I first heard the thing . . . I decided to speak this instead of the three cadenzas written for this work . . . Jesus is my elbow shit tonight! . . . Awake, overheated Apollo's temple! . . . O where is Zeppo when you need him most, all of them for that matter, the luftmenschen, all the bisbiglissando brothers of last season's subscription? You know, Harpo wasn't Harpo cause he played the harp, FYI — he's Harpo, mute Harpo, from Harpocrates, no joke, the god of silence, guardian of the rose of Eros. Manfred, the eldest, was to be the violinist, but he lived longer than all of us: he died in infancy like my sister after me, rendering me unto my parents as their only hope, and I'm your only hope, you who are leaving, going to coat-check and getting out of here, please wait, moment, langsam, shtum, please, psht — you know how much you paid for this, so sit down and enjoy the show if you haven't already refugeed and I don't know if I'd blame you if you did, I did, with my father and with my

Schneidermann

Schneidermann but without my mother because she was dead, dead like my younger sister, in younger infancy, dead like a child of mine too, I don't want to talk about it, dead like maybe Schneidermann is, I don't know, dead like I'll be soon, dead like this woman isn't, this woman I'd like to share with you, actually a letter, from a wife, never mine, not all of them are, a mother, here in a pants pocket, allow me to unfold it. It's from a woman I've never met — my present wife, which and whoever she is, has no grounds whatsoever for any of her accusations, and is her lawyer present? probably having drinks and eighteen holes with mine and mine's mine when I'd like to put eighteen holes in her — links always pursuing links . . . I received this letter from my agent, who, while he does nothing, does receive my mail. I'll leave off the salutation and some odd, touching personal details. And so the crux, originally from the Latin *cruciare, to torture*, reads:

> *Your music saved my life. I went through the worst of depressions: not eating, not sleeping, thinking serious about suicide, and you . . . your Beethoven Concerto, which I heard in Los Angeles last spring after my husband dragged me there, well, it made me want to live again. God Bless You . . .*

No. God Bless *You*, Agnes of L.A., Lamb of God, and thanks for writing, but God is dead, I have heard from a fellow countryman, but that doesn't mean I haven't done some good in someone's eyes, even though they may need multifocular glasses like mine, to speak through Spinoza's lungs of glass.

And

And then again, maybe she's a dog poisoner, or an arsonist, or a dues paid-up National Socialist, who knows? And who writes letters anymore anyway? Because who can read anymore anyway? But for a moment at least let's forget all that, the trash comes tomorrow morning at dawn so let's get to the essentials: who wants some cheesecake? some yummy in the tummy cheesy bakey-cakey-wakey-wakey those in the rear — and who doesn't want some? Everyone leaving, get some next door, on my tab, no problem — they'll file it against my estate. So eat up, enjoy before it all goes rotten, turns, turns, turns, and what the gehenna that exemplary passage? Additionally, allow me to recommend to you the fake cherry topping, or the coconut, decisions, decisions, decisions, and say a big hello to Kelli with an i or Kelly with a y there, the waitress with one eye gray and one eye brown. Women, what are they worth? Men, what are they worth? Music, what is it worth? This is undoubtedly the worst cadenza of my career. The first cadenza to Schneidermann was by a certain Kohen, the next by a Roubíček, listed in Patel's however as Roubicek — the latter heavily derivative of the former, R. of K. — both too virtuosic, Romantic, both friends of Schneidermann, false comforters to his Job. And me, I've got one of those love/hate's with the two poles, Romantic and Classical, but not Poles: I hate them all, except for a certain Jadwiga, but that's a long story I only half-remember . . . And I've recorded my own, thrice, it's published, two students of mine, hacks, play it often, consult your local media conglomerate for impertinent details. Kohen, though, who I met and attended his funeral, was an idiot, a man who devoted himself, and his career, to huge-German-M Modernity, because he wasn't

talented

talented enough to pull off the Classics, but I shouldn't talk: I listen to no music, and sometimes Bach, listen to him in my head, what retards refer to as the inner ear, hearing itself, right through the fuzz and the wax, though Noah — is Noah here? — the schmuck, he gifted me a stereo last Christmas, I never plugged it in, and what's it going to be this year, Noah? what else you got in your ark out in the suburbs? You know, I love Christmas here in Christendom, this Season of Seasons: that's been my most amenable, receptive hall, Christendom, excellent acoustics, though maybe too much capacity for reverb, and about capacity: where's the Fire Marshal when you need him? Too many law enforcers in our midst already, who called? a squad now, almost, in my sanctuary, the House which Heifetz built, and him, long dead, and only him, and Schneidermann, I'd bow to, and on second thought not Heifetz even, who also, the two of them, observed Christmas. Also the Heifetz I knew best, Larry Heifetz, owner of a great high-rated B&B down the shore, dead-end of the GSP, highly recommended but not for those cops in our midst who frankly couldn't afford it. Who's torn the pigs' tickets? Coat check anyone? Check your guns? Who exactly are you serving and protecting? Not Schneidermann you didn't when his apartment was broken into but admittedly there was nothing to steal. Not Schneidermann you didn't when he was mugged and the mugger found he had no money on him and so just knuckled a tooth out. Not Schneidermann you didn't when you fined him a hundred dollars he didn't have for smoking a cigarette he'd bummed off someone in the lobby of the Unemployment Office.

Schneidermann to me: the cops are after me.

Schneidermann

Schneidermann to me: the cops are after me because I'm an artist.

Schneidermann to me: they only come after the transcendent ones.

Schneidermann to me: they want to silence me.

Schneidermann to me: they have silenced me.

Schneidermann to me: I can't write anymore because that's just what the cops want me to do.

Schneidermann to me: where do I apply to become a cop?

Schneidermann to me: sirens are the most effective instruments of musical truth yet engineered by modern urban society . . . and it's thanks to him that I can name all of them, all the sirens, all by ear, shattering this winter, last night, lying atop my anonymous bed under the canopy, melting ice cubes on my bare chest, naked to the waist, a large dripping sponge, pooling in my bellybutton — yes, I have a bellybutton, I'm a man as much as anyone — my navel, sponge lying on my stomach, wrung out down to the bedspread, hell should be as hot as my room was, everything maxed-out, enormous industrial throb and the minifridge whining in Bb minor, then the shades kept it all out when day rose over ice, with the sirens passing by and me not being able to help myself: the police siren, the fire siren, the ambulance siren, the siren indicative of a heart attack, the siren indicative of cardiac arrest, the siren indicative of a shooting, the siren indicative of first-degree murder, second-degree, the siren indicative of manslaughter, the siren indicative of a passion murder (husband's murdering of wife being different sounding from wife of husband), the siren indicative of a burning accident, the siren indicative of a chemical accident, the siren

indicative

— 145 —

indicative of a car crash, of a five-car pile-up, the air-raid siren deep in my memory, the monthly tests scaring the hell out of everyone and I know them all, knew a trumpeter named Doppler, knew my European Humanism front to backwards and so it's probably from Socrates that I had this idea, the idea for this oration, last night, much like Plato's report of Socrates's final hours, his speechifying, and how, this is in the *Phaedon*, when Plato who wrote the thing in the third person says, so touchingly: "Plato, I think, was ill," but I was there, and I'm my own witness . . . baking under infinite artificial suns . . . me not to be confused with Dionysus, me not to be confused with Xenophanes, who was to never step over the horizon of a now specifically endearing mode of philosophy . . . the quivering string with the setting fingertip . . . he, Xenophanes, thinking that there were many suns just passing overhead, fingertips like successive suns passing over the horizon, and so maybe we do have the time allotted for me to massage your head with my callous calluses, what do you say to that? Xenophanes the rhapsodist, of Colophon, dimmed by the Homeric verses, denounced poets for giving Gods men's traits, anthropomorphizing them, and gave to the Greeks a single God, an eternal sphere, the earth's goatskin drum I'm pounding on. And I'm a rhapsodist too, but with no new innovation, no improved goods & services, just abusing public trust for what? for you? your sakes? I'm your somehow father? guide? Virgil? lover? Yes, you are all my Orphans and I, ladies and gentlemen, I am a liar's lyre thrumming some Thracian sweet talk. And can any uptown cunnilinguists enlighten me as to what in the gehennahell *harken* means and from what, wherefore and how is it so derived? But

I

I don't ask you to *harken*, merely to *listen*, to understand that it's not about imagination and the serial, or now whatever they've masked the serial as, it's not Apollo on one hand and Dionysus on the other — Apollo the bow, Dionysus the fiddle — no: it's all Orpheus, Apollo is Orpheus, Dionysus absolutely is, Orpheus in every hand, from the toes to the head, disembodied, singing still, and floating down the Hudson maybe. And Jesus, yes, and King David too, the tehillim you Reformim and unaffiliated schmucks in the midst of the encampment would refer to as the Psalms, all modeled on Orpheus. And so allow me to recall the *Hymns* of Thomas Taylor, his theme with variations of not a few fumigations. Can I get some houselights and what? You're calling maybe more police? SWAT? an army of lusty young men home from private wars? Overreact, it's fine with me — it was Orpheus I was orphing on and on . . . or die in sleep, that's the error of a waking man or some such Spinoza . . . and let's all now praise Alexander of Aphrodisias, may your ideas stand me in good stead tonight and ever rhapsodic after. May all your lives, your worthless petty lives, be as an infinite gliss up and down, infinitely up and infinitely down, an infinite piano keyboard played infinitely upon with infinite hands bearing infinite fingers of Bach's relatives, you know them? Who really wrote Mozart's *Requiem*? And Bach's debt to Buxtehude? — all these tinkerers of myths, interpreters of an enormous-German-C Culture and not just of a few dead white men. Like me. Understand? Priests and not a God, me and not Schneidermann. Schneidermann the last of the great unphonies and euphonies. Schneidermann the last of the great composers. Pythagoras to Schneidermann. Schneidermann to Pythagoras.

Pythagermann

Pythagermann. Schneidoras the last of the great. Schneidermann the last. Me, who deserves only to be torn apart — sparagamos I think it is dears, or maybe omaphagies, I forget — rend, ritually, this victim, or maybe I'm to be melon-scooped out by the women in my life, murdered by them with the implements of domesticity. You know, I've read, that the very same Plato hints at a cult of wandering priests who took money to relieve laymen from anxious guilt (check your ticket stubs): these were the Orphic priests. And then there's reincarnation: the flower that's not in my lapel, my boot-in-here. So please feel free to consider this an initiation ritual into manifold secrets, a schmeck of the Orientalism that destroyed not me. Because this is ritual and not a whole society's flight of fancy. Because this is art not some gross mistake. Because within this hall, within this violin, within me, are the secrets of Jesus and David and Solomon and every orb which shined with orph. Reasons they say and I say excuses. Time marches on they say and I say ensuring that the next generation doesn't drool another flood on the planet. I say further not original sin but a sense of loss from the first that my landsmen, my dead and once-slandered without-a-countrymen, explained much better than I could ever hope to, so I see that now you're listening, but this isn't an apology, or at least not yet. But I won't invoke names, no, no naming names unto the commission: because naming is owning, is possession, is eleven-tenths of any divine law pertaining thereto and anyway it's better to have every name, whatever people, the press, your wives, your children, want to call you: Polyonymos, asshole. I'm gonna tell you what you can and what you can't do, because God I don't believe in knows someone

has

has to, but first let us welcome the Chief of Police of this fine urbis and the Director of this wonderful hall coming down the center aisle as if for binding consecration at my hands, but I'm the one to be bound, no? Good evening, gentlemen, no irony in that, no, from me? Perhaps you know the work, Chief, of Ulrich von Wilamowitz-Möllendorf, no? O, but you should. Because Orphism in the Orphica was not a religion, but an art, understand? Because religion is art is philosophy is WHATEVER SATISFIES, maybe, like the candybar I like to eat but shouldn't, like the candybar I'd share with Schneidermann at the movies, like the candybar I'd buy for us at the movies but he'd eat the whole thing. And the Johnny Walker Red Label whiskey he'd bring for the Coca-Cola Classic, and the popcorn with something passing for butter, like the book he'd try to read in the light of the matinée movie: anything by Herodotos, anything by Damaskios, in the original. But separate me from my stalk and my head'll still be singing, floating in the perfumed midsts . . . my Greek was execrable, as was Shakespeare's . . . From them I learned that Orpheus birthed the Muse: her name to me was Alicia once and Maria tonight, and maybe Marketa, then Ashima and Allison and then lots of Alanas, Schwartz and Weisz, the latter a soprano and did I ever remember to you the joke? Orpheus and me, the "fathers of lays," as glossing Pindar. Because what was Orphic was every religion rolled into one, what we would know of now as the Western World, and you'd know me as one of its avatars, you'd know me as the avatar of avatars, you'd know me only if you'd listen but instead some of you are drinking a reception already. Langsam, you'll have your opportunity for rebuttal when I'm good and dead. But let's say

for

for argument's sake that it's a search for the mystical, the personal, you want. New-aging getting older, without grace, and what onyx saveths you now? Well it's too bad, to be denied you. Because *I* knew Schneidermann. Because I watered his ferns when he was away concertizing. Because I watered his daughters (dead in Birkenau) when he was away concertizing and lecturing. Who're you talking to Chief? Don't give me your megaphonics! No, *you* listen to reason! I watered his wife (dead in Birkenau) and his daughters when he was away concertizing and lecturing and teaching. No, I won't come down from the mountain until I've had my tablets, and I watered his wife and his daughters sometimes at the same time when he was away concertizing and lecturing and teaching and working: this was my practice, what one of my Ostland girls calls my *practicizing*, and, yes, I took my meds, my pills, yes I remembered and no, it has nothing whatsoever to do with that, come on, Doc Alan, and the rest of you keep smelting away at that calf now that I'm mixed like my meds, and where was I? With Orpheus. And who was he besides me? A hedgehog in foxfurs to babel his enemies, Trojaning them. Schneidermann, as difficult to place as Zeus: was He Chtonios *and* Olympios? did he change names like Schneidermann changed shirt collars? and changed names also: first his name, Schneidermann, and then later, over here in the underheated flat I have to sort out one of these days, Schneiderman, two *n*'s to one *n*, so which one was it or two? and once even on an American concert program three *n*'s, morons, and then what? Did the letters, the naming, make him any less of a mann or a man? Who knows? Capricious as Mozart he was, a composer he loathed and thought an inferior

imitation

imitation of God or C.P.E. Bach, but you have to forgive a man his idiosyncrasies, don't you? Especially a man who was raised, after his father died young, by his seven aunts. They were his real instructors. Goddesses all and he was a God. Because art and only art is "the authority for ritual," or so says Guthrie, you know him? A three-initialed scholar and his is a hieros logos. But what do I know? But everything, right? No, President Astoria the Third of this great hall erected on the aching spines of dead meatpackers and railroaded employees, this is not embarrassing, not a regrettable incident — I'm making an honest true spectacle of myself, up on this parquet mountain-top and finally, propitious, thank the Gods here are the house lights so I can look my devourers in the eye. But Orpheus, it is said, forbade cannibalism. So what are you going to do with so much flesh? Yes, I've put on a few pounds — shylock it, a good idea, but to who? — and no, you'd've noticed, my publicity shot's not quite up to date. Important to note, though, and understand, that fat people are essentially harmless. Schneiderman or Schneidermann himself was a spine with some skin on it, even through the fat years of banquets and tribute feasting when and where he ate like Fort, Dionysus, like the night in Berlin, 1936, at the Baron's who'd joined the Party not three days prior and that lapel pin of his, Schneidermann asked him where he got it from, that interesting four-pronged design, where could I get something like that?

Schneidermann to me: what are these mushrooms?

Schneidermann to me: shitake?

Schneidermann to me: no, they're ceps.

Schneidermann to me: no, not ceps, but definitely not shitake.

Schneidermann

Schneidermann to me: really, truly delicious, maybe boletus.

Schneidermann to me: no, on second thought, trompettes, shaped like the instrument, you get it? Like Gabriel's. Like Louis Armstrong's. Like the Baroness sneezing all night through those two fluted nostrils all stuffed up with seasonal sinus problems which wasn't necessarily a tragedy because even in those days Schneidermann smelled terrible. Which recalls to me a line of Guthrie's: "When a Neoplatonist quoted the Orphic writings, it was often to impart an aroma of antiquity to his doctrines." But you can smell under my armpit and I'm maybe not halfway through, smell me any day of the week for that matter, wake me up and smell me and put me down again and I smell incredibly springlike, it's the deodorant I wear but never anti-perspirant, my whole flanks are as white as the tundra, frozen for ten hours worth of protection in this freeze, guaranteed, twelve hours of protection, twenty-four even and what time is it anyway? Not that it matters. Music itself stops time: Orpheus there singing and strumming, time suspended, the music of the spheres, Joshua at Gideon with the sun stilled. But time is a way of enlisting two ideas in mutual defense, dialectics. I'm of German extraction (that's what Oma put in her soups, secret ingredient of German Extract), and with this definition of time we'll be able to divine the proof for my theory that art and religion never flourish at the same time, no, think about it for a second that's not a second and that doesn't even exist in the first place, not the front row, front lines, where all of you have too much money and not enough time. Because it's time I've wasted pulling the dialectic apart, ritual rending apart of the intended victim, between on the one

gnarled

- 152 -

gnarled, soon Parkinson's probably hand the enraged Maenads and on the other, the Muses. And which will Maria be? Depends if I ever intend on returning to the Grand, if I can get any work after this. If I can even get home unassisted after this. If I'll ever get home. Usher, you of winged Hermes, why do you flee fleet? Sacred, winged, fickle things, why are you never tipped? Here's some money for you — come and catch, or we'll put it in escrow. No, don't grab — it's for them: thank you all O so very much for your unrivaled expertise in the field of alphabetical order and numberology: seating plans tattooed on your fore-arms, which makes me think of Schneidermann and how it was before the Cadenza of History, before the improvised history, what set me against my beloved Romanticism. Understand that when the world is Romantic the art is Classical and vice-versa, that they each think the other and read your Nietzsche with sunglasses that aren't your prescription (Schneidermann's memory was great because his eyesight was terrible, sense-of-smell and hearing too, believe it, everything). Reminds me of black & white, childhood, all that with the tattoo on the drums and the march into Märchen, history *in an improvised style*: one egotist soloing on the instrument of humanity (sawing away: a magician?), one man above all the rest playing with all of us in an improvisatory style, and not just that, but really improvising, sure, there're some tropes: mass-death anyone? One full of himself man improvising, playing with history with insufferable panache, real admirable technical brilliance, virtuosity even, an overload, a superabundance of brilliance, which is disaster. Don't you feel, not you, don't answer, that some periods, eras, are made up on the spot, extemporized and that you're the

material

material being manipulated? We, me and Schneidermann, were high notes in Hitler's, one European's Cadenza of History, the upper spectra of the tessitura. Though Schneidermann went through the camps, all the camps, and I went through nothing in London. Schneidermann, I remember now, with this need, the idea of shit, of artistic excess, his piano throne with the built-in custom toilet so that he'd never have to stop playing, yes, playing — playing being the ultimate thought — and then the roll he'd prepared inside the piano, resting on the strings roundabout C4, explosive! Did I say I'm a terrorist and Jesus does that put a scare into you! Terrorist or Good Shepherd, it's the same gig. Because uprights were all he played over here. Why? One reason is money. Though he went to occasional parties, up near Columbia Gem of a University, a block from Bartók, near Gershwin's and Mozart's grocer, he was more feared (respected) than loved (respected). Because it's Homer the professor who gets all the medals and not Orpheus the artist, it's always the public intellectual half-raped into existence (that's the meat of the Upper West sidetalk) from a windblown seed renting out either the aither or the ether at what he couldn't afford, and that's what they used, the ether, when Schneidermann had his spleen out, which he also couldn't afford to and to not to, letting me have a piece of it, and I ate it, and it leaves lesions on the mental apparatus like playing, or even listening to, the goddamn A-whining oboe four-hundred-and-forty-times per moment however defined. The Sirens and Orpheus the sailor, like me and Schneidermann on his ship (my father getting Jew-sick below), the weakling artist with no sea legs under him, because legs are unnecessary for an artist,

because

because an artist must be weightless, sailing in your skull's vessel across the wide ocean, ergo nought. And finally silencing the Sirens, subduing them, and so we have three tropes: Sirens and Muses and Mother May Nads, and which was which, and which brother-in-law or overbearing father loosed his snake unto my Eurydice, name meaning *wide-ruling*, I've read, and did they ever rule wide! as the ocean, iron-fisted from behind iron curtains they took me to task forever, ewig, how did the woman get so strong on this side of the ocean? Because it used to be fathers we were afraid of, read your K., okay, I'm sure you have, unfortunately, K. not as in Mozart, but as in my father, my adopted father while my real father was still alive, my false Schneidermann — an incredible taskmaster, phylactery whips — he was a religious artist, a worker of incredible hours of incredible discipline, all self-imposed. Because I just couldn't be trusted, could I? Because I told more lies than a husband all that was left for me was to run up and down my scales, scaling my scales: *do*, *re* and *me* at quarter note equals prestississississississis-sissimmo, off the metronome's scale, scaling higher and faster, a warped metronome on his windowsill overlooking the garden, warped and slowed and that's how I became so much of an interpreter. But I want to be the speaker, like you, Chief, yes, that's it, take a seat, finally. Someone get him some coffee, two creams and two sugars, but if you leave the hall, please, I beseech you, save your stubs. Because outside is the descent into Hades, hell, and Orpheus returning empty-handed after shystering the death god, Schneidermann, who you thought was Zeus, but didn't I tell you you didn't know from truth? That phantom of a woman, a shadow of a shade. Whisked away

because

because I made a mistake, so shoot me, seriously, I failed huge, and I'm sorry, I relent and repent being but ashes from dust to dust, striking my tit in the gesture of indigestion or repentance. The failure though, a late addition, like the Florida room Number Two, a parlor really and as stifling, she had added on to the house in Miami where all the rooms are Florida rooms and then she goes and shtups the workmen she hires, and all because I shtupped her sister, well, listen: mistakes were made. And her sister was her: they looked the same in the dark, which is why you can't trust your eyes, especially my eyes, only your ears, your hearing, and my ears they knew it wasn't her, my wife, but someone else, maybe from the pitched moaning or the cries and utterances and imprecations or maybe because she cried, uttered and imprecated another man's name, her husband's, who's a good man, into insurance, which is what I need right now like a hole in my head, which brings me back to my original point, my ur-request (my Isaac to Schneidermann's Abraham), that someone should seriously, at least seriously consider the possibility of shooting me. Not meaning take my photograph. In my overburdened and overtaxed head: you know what I pay in income and property taxes down there in Florida? No, it's the Alexandrians who came up with the failure angle on Orpheus: they had that pathetic spirit, that empfindsamkeit-deal. Charon or Sharon was her name, the pathetic one, the yoga farter and yes, yes, yes I've urinated in my pants. Because I can't leave, can I? Diaper the diapason and always remember Aristaeus, Euridyce's, the Thracian nymph's or Dryad's, undesired lover: he was my manager, my agent, the guy who scoops the gorgeous autumn out of my lap pool leaf by

sogged

sogged heavy leaf. But do you even know the names of trees? No, and so they're not yours! Trees inclined to sweet music to help them grow, and then the animals gathered and were subdued. Do I need to hold up a mirror? Surely some of you have mirrors in your purses, maybe compact roundlings to reflect the stage lights in my eyes so I can't see anymore and only hear. O but I see you've killed the stage lights! and right on cue, bravo lighting maestro who shtups his little moisturized hands up in the misted booth, yes, a masturbator. Orpheus too shunned the company of women for men or celibacy or music or death: the same things. And I'm there soon enough by the banks of the Strymon, by the banks where all my accounts have been frozen like wives. I'm now Baroque, who's going to fix me and what's it going to cost? Frozen like my now untended pool, like the unsalted sidewalk outside HAMU in Prague, their conservatory, where I slipped and broke a hip and you don't want those doctors — so you see, contrary to my doctor's recommendations (and they're only recommendations) all you need is salt in the wounds of any ego, because that's what conservatories offer: there's always someone better, faster, more talented, engineering you (not me) out of service. But that was then. Now most music students have no ability to express anything musical on an instrument or with their voice, defective musical hearing, and some have, actually, actually unsurprisingly, no real interest in music as music. They can't sing a simple melody or improvise an accompaniment to a folk tune or even reproduce a simple pop song, but they talk, O how they talk about the musical language of Late Beethoven as if his name was not Ludwig but Late, Late van Beethoven, or about aleatorics or

stochastics

stochastics, I don't know, and that's because music's no longer in their blood, in our blood, in blood. A Jesus Bach chorale has forsaken us. And dodecaphonic music, 12-tone music, is dead. Atonality is dead. Music is dead. And the retards win. No disrespect intended to the wheelchairs on the floor. Will you please rise and I'm just joking — the metaphoric retards I mean, you have to be peesee, politically correct and incorrect in their own, respective and always respectful, seasons, have to be fair to each of J. J. Fux's five species, of counterpoint, polyphony, rudiments of composition, which study, the *Gradus*, formed the basis of almost every great 18th- and 19th-century composer's education. And when huge-E Early van Beethoven's Fux-based studies with Haydn's friend Albrechtsberger were translated into French by the great musicologist Joseph-François Fétis in 1833 (six years after Early's early death), you wouldn't believe whose names showed-up on the list of subscribers: Cherubini, Berlioz, the Jew Meyerbeer, Chopin, Rossini, Auber, Paganini, that converted Jew Moscheles, Hummel and Liszt and on and on to some names long since decomposed on their own, decomposing without the (though appreciated) assistance of your, of everyone's, vast ignorance. Because musicians must teach the next generation (though I don't well), and any education obtained basically on your own, or unneeded (like mine), is nothing less nor more than however well-intentioned revisionist history. But now, deceptively, recordings are supposed to teach, technologies teach, though everyone quick to employ them are equally quick to admit that nothing's an acceptable substitute to something they (equally) will never mention, nor themselves experience: life, and not this updated

Kappellmeisterism

Kappellmeisterism Version 2.0. Jay-Jay Fux: "Since God is the highest perfection, the harmony composed for his praise should follow the strictest rules that perfection can claim, as far as human imperfection can realize them." A fine sentiment, but practically worthless — all Bach's fugues don't satisfy the rules passes for wisdom around here and everywhere else in Fux's faux-Socratic Q&A format, but: "As the number of voices increases, the rules may be less rigidly observed," and that's what ends it, the work, what puts a stop to what works, let's say, in a cinematic context, look: Beethoven didn't get along with Haydn, wasn't given enough attention, that spoiled child, felt he wasn't given enough attention, and so he turned to Albrechtsberger. Beethoven, writing among his assignments: "Albrechtsberger told me today that there are some works by the old master Froberger in which the use of the fourth, even that occurring by inversion of the triad, is completely avoided. This was done because the perfect triad, as symbol of the Holy Trinity, was to be maintained with absolute purity." — But there's absolution and then there's maintenance, like when they had to redo the cracked bell over at St. Vitus in Prague, after it died and predicted the hundred-years' flood, a bell tolling now, midnight for us. And so hark and hear the distant church on the other side of the ocean, its bells soon striking our midnight, their six in the evening, when they're all salting their meat plates and guzzling beer.

Because I had friends there: Braunstein, Schwarzstein, Grabstein, and the slide into what followed . . .

Die Posaunenstelle

Die Posaunenstelle

But Gabriel's gone isn't he? And his part with him.

tief im glühenden Lit. trombone but in Luther's a trumpet, Cf. Apoc.

Leertext, but what exactly is missing and am I to be his redactor?

in Fackelhöhe, and what's this funny business with the lights, anyway?

im Zetiloch: which is where we are, not to be too obvious, after the music stops.

hor dich ein, yes, do that . . .

mit dem Mund, with anyeverything and the mouth, a pack of lips, apocalypse, and music is the Zeitloch, voids of interpretation and the actual weighed in the scales of our ears . . . aaaaahhhhhhh . . . in which the ear hearing itself, the hear earing itself in the plunkings and scrapings of my fellow students at the conservatory, that which conserves that which is neglected by everyone else. I hear Braun, later the streetsweeper. Schwarz, later the undertaker, grabbing you and sticking you in the wet mud, graving you on the earth, imagine that. But that was Paul, not Peter that thrice denier, and he too was one of us, Antschel and then Ancel and then Celan, an Amsel high above a suicide in Paris. A great admirer of Schneidermann and admiration returned, but, let's just say some postage was due. B. the pianist and S. the clarinetist, but what's this? — the house lights up and down again? What's this about? What's the program? or there'll be no encore. Whatever you say Mister Hall President, Astoria great name? get what? A Handel on myself, hahaha, you know, Petro Esquire, Handel's father, a barbering surgeon,

wanted

wanted him to be a lawyer, but lucky for us, you shyster Petro sitting with the Chief, and Mister Arschstoria President — your sold-out hall at curtain is now either half-full or half-empty depending, and if you ask me it's the latter for the very reason that I'm not a homosexual but a pessimist. And so Schneidermann's fate then, because what we're interested in, here, are fates, and fates only. Because what do lives matter? Nothing. Amount to? Efes. All prophets should end up denying their Gods — so take a long walk Schneidermann, like you always did, hands clasped behind your back, Brahms (Beethoven's battered wife), and that day you disappeared — was that a totem in your pocket or were you just happy to see me? or is that question taboo? I should know to have the answers — after all, I am to you what Horace, not Greeley, said of Orpheus, said he was: *Sacer interpresque deorum*, the sacred interpreter of the Gods, and as such I address you directly. Orpheus, the man almost god who dies — ever hear that spiel before? But Orpheus wasn't like Jesus H. — no, Jesus wasn't a singer, more a mamele's boy, a castrato like Haydn almost was, though, as Lefranc de Pompignan notes, he was Orpheus *the first of the world's singers*, in poems earlier than Homer's. Schneidermann's first teacher was a man named Schneidermann, the boy's father, dead, and then his next teachers, Schneidermanns too, his father's seven sisters, the seven musical aunts who raised him, muses too and, yes, I'm implying incest not of Krafft-Ebing's idealized sort, but dirty, dirty, dirty origins of this *mystagogue* (one of his favorite words in his newest language), this synoptic man and his synoptic religion, a religion of art, kind of a Gesamtkunstwerk of

enormous-

enormous-German-L Life — and how're your foreign-tongued chops feeling tonight? O, I wish he were here tonight! — how he'd explain it all to you, so Bach crystalogic, and, well, let's summon him up, shall we? An Upper West Side séance of sorts, lets rap the tables of your diamonds set in your gold rings, shall we? — and see, no hear, what he's up to? Maybe a timpani for this on the tympanum? But no. Because how I'd hear it when I was on tour, later, was through the magnificent invention of distanced speech, a sort of extrasensory perception by which I of course mean the telephonic apparatus. O, how I touch myself to the moist heavy sound of the dial tone and the young, lonely operator. Now let us praise the telephone's inventors: Philipp Reis, Antonio Meucci, Elisha Gray and not to forget Mister Alexander the Great Nevsky, gram for gram the greatest man of his time and on his dime. His, Schneidermann's, was an early century model still in work, still at work (we're talking something like Siemens & Halske here), but funny thing about it was you couldn't hear through it — in another word he could only talk, as someone called him and he picked it up, had to guess who it was, or not, or just not care, and he'd just start talking, monologing, ranting, sermonizing to desert rabble. He'd call someone — sometimes he couldn't remember who by the time the other party picked up — and he'd just start going off again. But he couldn't hear a gottesdamned ding with his accent anyone on the other side was saying and when they hung up, then he hung up. So if I got lonely and just wanted to hear, I called him and he gave me my piece of his mind and then when I had had enough, I hung up, and then, I guess, he did too — easy enough, didn't trouble his own house, you know? And he never

called

called women, thinking the telephone too crude to use to call
women — it was for men to discuss absurd, weighty things,
issues, you know? And often he'd hum or sing or read his translations of Shakespeare into a language he invented and only he
understood — so who knew if they were actually translations?
Or he'd rest the receiver down on the piano's lid and he'd play:
synesthetic Scriabin, whom he was smart enough to admire,
and Beethoven, forget the late sonatas, yes, he played only his
own keyboard arrangements of Beethoven's symphonies and,
if your ring rang late at night, left-handed whorehouse piano
in the late style, four-five ante meridian, with updated performance practice meaning dead drunk, and thank you for
keeping your telephones at home, phones which ring only in
the key of SEE, when you arrived promptly at this whorehouse
this evening, or else he'd pull a fugue out of his arsch, and FUG
as in fleeing from his own forehead he'd hold against the keys
and beat the keys' lid against, on his neck like a guillotine, when
he got stuck for an academic Mahler, screw-you Apollonian
brothers stretto or a development modulating to other things,
so many of them that made him smash his throat with the keys'
lid: Asians, Asians, Homosexuals, Single Old Women who
Owned More then One and sometimes only One Cat, Students
of Philosophy, Happy Paraplegics, Young Men, Young Men,
Young Men, Men Younger Than Himself Not Excluding Me,
Poets in Languages No One Spoke . . . but he envied them and
that was, the envy, the source of his hatred, yes hatred, and
smashing . . . And his brother . . . Because his aunts murdered
his brother when they were pushing his, Schneidermann's,
piano, a grand, like my hotel, unlike what he had over here (an

upright

upright), pushing it, the grand, or maybe baby, across the room to have better dappled light for the young prodigy's practice and study and they pushed with too much energy, pushed too far, and the piano went right out the large floor to top window of the apartment on the top floor . . . dorfer with the extra key, and this was in Budapest on a street that no longer exists, or now in hiding under an assumed name, and the piano shattered out of it and fell six stories crushing and killing his, Schneidermann's, younger and only brother, also twin, a totally unmusical personality named Rudy, even though he was of the same religion as, and killing him forever . . . pedals: una corda, sostenuto, damper and the kid's school-stockinged feet stuck out from underneath like in what's it called? Oz, fell like losing pitch to that which is Most High, a string constantly tuned higher and higher until it snaps on the sidewalk with a sound that was like the atom bomb, which was a handful of years later, actually 25/5ths of a handful later, and which he, Schneidermann, Rudy's older brother, claimed ruined his hearing forever after — so that might be your telephone answer right there, and the issues with the late Beethoven resolved easy, neat and simple like a Zarathustrian dominant to tonic, the buzzing pedal like of the bicycle young Rudy would ride unfettered and free, the healthy youth, the one half alive while Schneidermann, half dead, stayed pale and inside and *practicized* and didn't play well with the other children, but *played with himself* — they didn't even know he existed, yet, and maybe not after and half because they were twins, Schneidermann, our and my Schneidermann, one whole minute older, and in that minute he came to know and perfectly

understand

understand, to perfectly know, this large and imperfect world where things happen like seven aunts unknowingly, in which they're trying to do some good, killing one of two nephews, the sons of their one dead brother, the boys' father, but it must be said, put on record, that they loved Rudy much less than they loved Schneidermann, ours and mine, and so there was maybe something unconscious at work, but who knows because by then Freud was at the other polar end of the Continent and his students, well, most of them, Schneidermann's friends, would have forsaken him, Freud, by then, for something less fantastic, more mature. And the piano umpteen six stories fell, Rudy squashed, huge strings and loosened keys not tumbling head over heels like lovers fall, but falling, straight down, a virtuoso fall, a true plummet, the sound an anthropomorphized pluck of an infinitely tuned string strung to a heavenly sphere — yes, it almost pulled the dead sun down with it, with the mammoth shatter: a rill up and down infinite as Rudy was riding his bicycle and, yes, eating a banana, peel on the sidewalk, man on the corner saw it and cried! his trenchcoat draped over a puddle for his ladyfriend (then you had ladyfriends) . . . and it hit! legs buckled, pedals stuck out from under like feet, accordion squash, dead squeezebox — but I wasn't there — sides split, tensions exploded off of tuning pegs, lids bucked, women wept freely into their lace handkerchiefs as their husbands held them around their thick necks, looked at their watches as you're doing now, the final chord, resolution of the cadence, dominant to tonic, perfect and authentic, curtain, applause, curtain, bow, curtain, all contrapuntal and then this is elision, to dark, sharps and flats of enharmonic night, the black-black-black-keys, night

falling

falling with the piano until the continent entire was void —
someone fire me from a cannon to saw away in mid-air say in
the ballpark of Adagio or Largo, slow. Because the thing hit!
And the noise it filled history, inflated the past with sound
we can hear if we listen. If we listen to the right people. If we
listen to Bach. If we listen to Mozart. If we listen to Beethoven.
If we listen to the early speeches of the great and surely
immortal Adolf Hitler. But have you been listening to anything
I've been saying? Has the world mislaid its brain? Left its
mental apparatus in its other pants? Because he, Schneidermann,
to his detriment, had read, had memorized, his Walter Pater
— Schneidermann's life constantly aspired to the condition of
music, unfixed, much mechanics. This Pater quote from *The
School of Giorgione*, anyone hungry? and published in the year of
Schneidermann's father's birth, 1873, year amid another
Renaissance for us Jews . . . And Schneidermann, O
Schneidermann! born out of date, unborn of date, stillborn in
too fastening a time, quicksilver — like these fingers, my entire
life, four fingers applied to four strings, wood and some metal,
guts, like the death of their God, of the man who thought he was
a God, the God who thought He was a man, and of course some
right hand sawing, masturbation. Speed I have, but an old form
of speed, analog before analog, outdated — like what they say
about Szigeti's vibrato, you know? Szigeti, a true God of the
violin and his name should be gilt up there and not Heifetz's.
We need anything to get ourselves out of this computer sound
(*computer* such a last season word), this digitizedsoundworld or
whatever Germanisch monster, this impersonal lushness, his
corporate warble — and, truth be told, sacrilege, that's my

final

final answer on Heifetz. Because you should've heard me — I should've heard myself on a 78. Understand that too often the idea is the beauty and intensity of the violin rather than the expressive flesh of the music. Invoking all this, these ideas of interpretation, allow me to interpret a ghost in the darkness, a play on the stage of another play, one stage of evolution giving way to our more accomplished, happier ancestors no longer around to take a bow, to meet a curtain's call. I once took a bow — some Baroness lent it to me and I never returned it after the tour, it suited me, and she didn't want to disturb the natural order of things, because the rich preserve dignity, however false and rotten it might be, what else you think keeps my traveling healing show, well-snake-oiled, on the road? But I, and Schneidermann, born poor. And we took to ascension, elevation, loft. Me, after or now they say post, Kreisler and Flesch, Elman and Huberman, Menuhin — great violinists, as liner or program notes go, of the interwar years, before the Cadenza of History. Me too, even in those days, a marketable prodigy, short pants so my putz would stick out the leg when I sat, and so I stood, and played. Szigeti, and I, the same trajectory: Budapest, Royal Academy or by then the Franz Liszt Academy of Music, then to Berlin and Busoni, who taught him music, took him from the flash (in the pan) of display pieces, the schlocky salon melodies, prodigy repertoire, stock-in-trade . . .

Because most virtuosos spend more time practicing and learning, memorizing the once-improvised cadenza than they do the concerto. Cadenzas are so codified as to be as lasting as the true composed work, yet cadenzas have no form but ego, masturbation, ego-masturbation, ergo rendering the

cadenza

cadenza the perfect form, (non-form), for our times. Because a cadenza's a form that isn't a form. Cadenza, a non-form that's also a form. Cadenza, a painstakingly constructed ruin. Cadenza, calculated abandon. Cadenza, planned recklessness. Cadenza, calculated recklessness. Cadenza, planned abandon. Cadenza . . .

THE CHILDREN'S CHORUS

O, so I see they've schlepped in my kinder. Subway'd them to midtown. How many of you have been here before? fixed the place up nice didn't they? I have as many as Bach, I think Wilhelm F. and C.P.E. and Johann G.B. and by Anna Magdalena: Elisabeth and Johann C.F. and Johann C., all grand-kids of old Hans Bach who had a son, no joke, hand to God, named Lips, died all of 1620. But mine, all they do is give lip. Hello there! Yes, I hear you. Amiel and Ariel or. What's your name, no don't tell me. Nathaniel and Shimon, and by Sumi, Akira, now Akira what's the new one's name? What? Repeat it for me, slow, hearing's not what it used to be. Akira Goldberg. Lord. That's my alphabet wherein G is followed by A, the enhar-monic note, G#/Ab, in the middle responsible for a sort of light blue phenomenon. How have you all been, how's life been treating you and no, I won't come to my senses, no I won't come down and be reasonable. How's the new gig, Joshua? Treating you well? And the wife? I hear through to remain anonymous socialites of the Upper East variety that you have three children now, so I'm multiplying as a grandparent. But how far do you reasonably expect my love to spread? Like

creamed

creamed cheese over warmisch pumpernickel, I need a nickel, a dime spared, I need everything I can get my grubby Jew hands on! hahaha, the nerve, the nerve to have so many children, to weigh down this world with more replicas, drones, lessening imitations of love which doesn't even touch down to my naked toes. Schneidermann would answer the door nude, a faddish Austro-Hungarian thing, a Wandervogel nature-idea, but still? Unembarrassed, natural as anything, he'd admit you in. That was my best performance, one New York afternoon, me and him at his piano, her, an upright as he, believe it. Way the gehenna and gone uptown. Not a piano reduction, even on his reduced piano, but he nailed down everything. The orchestra — which has slowly dispersed behind me, all except for the baby timpanist who seems to find me amusing, don't you? — well, Schneidermann held your whole woodwind section in his right ring finger, unadorned, unmarried like Glenn Gould but Schneidermann was a more formidable pianist (as was Richter), was a more formidable everything. Ask the woodwind section: the years of training, of discipline, fine honing and for the oboes, reed insanity, the money that bought them, you, the leisure to fine hone — because there are no geniuses here — he, Schneidermann, had all that above the knuckle. How could you — dispersed backstage, into cabs or subways and away, statements to the press, next door for teas to watch me up on the screen, gossip — how could you expect to live? If you even wanted to? If you weren't staying on this thing — I'm sweating too much, sweating on you, sorry — if you weren't staying on this road because there hasn't yet been a turnoff, a welcomed detour? Like the road — if it could be called a road — I took

from

from Bukovina to Budapest and I hitched and walked that, to my first lesson with Schneidermann, no, truth, with a famous violinist, a virtuoso, and there I roomed with the virtuoso's nephew (to remain nameless) in one room and studied in the afternoon with Schneidermann, in his studio like India, like I thought India would be like, like India wasn't when I finally made it there for a benefit but as it should have been. Because I moved from the virtuoso to the musician, the hack to the artist, switched studios (something you never do!), declared allegiance to music over shit, art over shit, God over shit, in the end redeeming shit over unredeeming shit, in the end transcendent shit over mundane shit, meaning over gesture, the shit of meaning over the shit of gesture, and there was only one among us who was not a monkey flinging around its own shit, who wasn't a retarded child eating his own shit, dead in childhood from eating his own shit, reincarnated as a spider monkey flinging around its own shit, a lemming — you ever encounter one of those? — for sins too numerous and too grievous to apologize for just now, to atone, repent, or so it seemed, then.

Busoni to Szigeti as Schneidermann to me: You Must Be Man Enough To Realize Your Own Mistakes! but it sounds better in the original. You must be genius enough to claim, to believe, to know your mistakes are better than what you do correctly! (The faithleap of the great soloists: Hitler, Stalin, Caesar, Alexander . . .) And this the essential change, metamorphosis if you like, from Prodigy to Man. Innocence, understand, brooks no mistakes. Your sister broke Bubbe's dish (not you, Leah, I'm talking about my life), even if you don't have any sisters, are an only child and you have a concert to think about

in

in three hours for rich patrons your father wants to know better. Mistakes, understand, make it all the more correct. And so, let's set up the dialectic now, indulge me: Ysaÿe parted the waters of Joachim (expression) and de Sarasate (technique), united it, according to Flesch (my flesh was dead, or not yet born), by making vibrato, that adam's apple shake, an essential component of style — vibrato, an artful inaccuracy. Kreisler shook it out, further, using vibrato, employing it even in fast passage work. And now, with my arms and hands and fingers giving me problems, the carpal tunnel vision that I have and arthritic putz, everything hurting, I can't even be a retarded monkey anymore. My arms hurting and my wrists and my hands and my pointer, my index, my fuck-you finger and my ring and my pinkie and all their joints and knuckles ache, and so I have to remove myself from the zoo before all the bad reviews begin flowing. Before my chordophone's taken away from me, repo'd, impounded and all, I can take a stand! from the first violin section most probably. Rests. Shut up Stephen! — I always hated you because you look too much like your mother, but without the breasts, and what a tailpiece on her too, when she was young. Not like my Frieda, who she just slept all day — this was my first woman, the woman who cleaned Schneidermann's house, or who was supposed to clean it but never did, she just slept, and drank huge cups of scalding, steaming hot tea, teacups so enormous day after day they'd hide her face, so huge you couldn't, after a month of the illness which killed her, you couldn't get into her room, was as if the teacup was blocking ingress and egress, and the heat! She had an important job in the Schneidermann house —

which

which she never did — and yes, Marc, I know I've told this story a thousand and one times, she was supposed to be able to differentiate between butcherpaper to be thrown out, and butcherpaper which held useful musical sketches, and, Jesus! she must have thrown out the equivalent of twenty-one sonatas, and I don't know why I pick that number . . . *ppp* . . . Because the heel of the bow, right here, is called the *frog* and that's what she called me and I don't know why . . . but maybe it's because I licked her so well before I betrayed her for her younger sister, who was hired when she, Frieda, got sick, to clean Schneidermann's house — or maybe her, the younger sister, was the one named Frieda, who remembers? great steaming cups of tea from Turkey so hot you'd never touch them to get near them arrayed around her bed to come in and clean for her, the girl whoever she was he, Schneidermann, paid for cleaning, and, I admit, the girl I paid for my first experiences and children, do you like to hear that? But later I just cleaned her room in exchange for favors, by the end just a quick tooth-some suck, and to clean the whole Schneidermann household — whichever then Misses Schneidermann and her daughters were lazy good-for-not-much, and weren't even awed by his — and to clean the whole thing but to never, ever, ever, never . . . these were Schneidermann's instructions, the only words he ever spoke to the Friedas, whom I did *mit Holz*, to: *never, ever, ever, never dust the piano or its bench*, which, the bench, of course doubled as his, Schneidermann's, toilet. And sick, and I think the both of them sick and with teacups, handles bursting through windows to stumble passersby in shards on the street — they slept as all European girls slept too much (Rilke) —

what

what gigs these girls had! like the scam Schneidermann's neighbor was working, a man who was cheating on his wife with his cleaning lady, the man was a civil servant of some sort who knows and he told his wife he was out late at night taking piano lessons from Schneidermann, two-three in the morning, soontime, time in another dimension, the past, and this man paid Schneidermann to keep up his cover, paid him, supported Schneidermann between commissions, never, and all Schneidermann had to do was to play piano late, which he did anyway, and it never annoyed his neighbor, the man's wife, because she thought that it was her husband taking his lessons, shows what she knew, and Schneidermann, though the man didn't ask him to, would say to the man's wife when he happened upon her in the street: *You know Frau Whatsoever, your husband's really coming along. His Verbinski Sonata is quite accomplished considering how long he's been playing.* — which is funny, one because it's not true and two because there was never a composer named Verbinski, Schneidermann made it up, or at least no famous composer known to me as Verbinski, and I would know, I would think, and so no sonata numbered even Opus Zero. But one time this man and his wife were at a society party and the wife of the host asked this man's wife to ask her husband to entertain them on the spinet and she asked and he had to say to her, an excuse later repeated to Schneidermann the next Wednesday when he paid him and they played chess, which Schneidermann always won even when he handicapped himself without one of the rook's pawns and he, Schneidermann, always playing Schwarz . . . he, the man, said: *I'm sorry, but my teacher, Herr Schneidermann, has forbidden me to play in public until*

such

such time as he feels that I'm adequately prepared or somesuch thing like that: *and you know I'm so eager, but Herr Teacher must be respected* and they: *He knows what's right* . . . and the man and Schneidermann laughed, while the wife and hostess were disappointed, and apparently said as much to the man, this most probably tone-deaf man: *What a disappointment!* — Schneidermann's reputation as an eccentric was only heightened, and of course this man went on shtupping his cleaning lady, not Maria, at some hotel or at her, the maid's, blind and deaf grandmother's house, until he got syphilis, and Schneidermann was anyway never invited to these parties because once he was caught at one early in his career, in the linen closet at an after-concert party thrown by a real live from the grim fairy tales Princess, and also the toilet . . . could never control his outbursts . . . but this isn't for polite company such as my Leah here . . .

THE CHILDREN'S CHORUS

You remember my sins, don't you, Leah dear? Yes, I've noticed you out there, too much makeup as always and your gold's blinding me. But Shayna's the prodigy, and girl prodigies sell, I tell you, your daughter . . . Leah who's now, in later life, a failure who raises funds for what or whom? Leah Weiss now, many times divorced, and who doesn't want to Lay a Weiss? O, the perfection of childhood, the perfect innocence, the maturation — maturation is improvisation, Shayna, if you're listening, growing up. But women, forget it: it takes a man to know his mistakes, to love them — those are my true wives,

and

and I've evidently paid my alimony, must make a note, which one? to thank my manager, but no time now. Leah, how's husband # one thousand and nine treating you? flat daughters and a sharp mother, O but he's here too! the husband numbered late opuswise, slinking, disappearing towards the back of the house, fire exits illuminated even with the house lights on, off, on, or just the spot on me, in my house, it's my goddamned house, understand, you'll never take it away, you spoiled little squirts of dreck, you shitkopfs, ingrates and Philistines. Jesus, let's ask him, get his opinion, yes, why the F-hole not? Okay, are you, Doctor Weiss, and how have you been feeling, have you been feeling, lately? Might I borrow your prescription pad for a moment, a rest or two? I'd promise I'll return it, but you married my daughter — no, you, shhhhhhhhhhhh, ppppppppppppp . . . *hear* the dynamic markings, *mit Dämpfer* while you're at it — quite high-nosed she's become, Judiths, but is she in possession of any talent whatsoever? No, I wasn't around long enough to find out. And there are no encores? Listen, listen, listen — I almost fell, no, no help, you just stay — I'm going to die, I want to die, free, alone. Here's my handkerchief, can you catch? like a dove. Noah in his ark, watching golf on the screen wide as a raven's wingspan. I should have sold out, wish I thought of that earlier. I should've been a rabbi, a priest, a monk, mystic, hermit. Yes, yes, boo and heckle those few remaining adherents of this dying Yeshiva, crumple up those programs and throw them at me — I'm a good catch for those goodly hearkened days of old of short centerfield. But instead, I apply pressure to allow sounds, fingers on the tightrope like Saint Szigeti, patron of no one and nothing,

working

working the German circus, the Hungarian summer theater troupe — once in a Hungarian year, we once joked, would what happen? come to pass? 1913 and Szigeti gets TB, has to spend three Swiss years taking the cure, now we have the disease of Perlman and Zuckerman and whomever, Kremer maybe or, I don't know, don't even listen anymore, my landsmen. And so, working the worst gigs, there wasn't that false ascension, just the seamless uninterruption between Szigeti's prodigy and adult careers. You understand that unlike Jascha, Mischa, Sascha, he never appeared as an adult under his prodigy name: Joska, but always, and don't you forget it, as Joseph Szigeti. Knowing Schneidermann, a modern composer whatever that means, bit of the infant terrible to him, made me hate that prodigy life, discontent with standard repertoire and so on. Because the idea's to intuitively get to the heart of the piece, the heart of the heart of the heart, a passage, a goddamned note, as no one else, and you need to be able to circus it up, need to be open to improvising, experiment, to always approach fresh, new, unorthodox fingerings like me and Schneidermann's which wife? Because Flesch had warned long time ago of the monotony obtaining in thoughtless applications to all musics of an exaggerated vibrato, improper, nauseous stuff: "Blatantly sensuous, artificially inflated rather than naturally matured, spirit of our times . . ." Szell writing to Szigeti: "Any subtle function of the wrist and fingers of the right hand is practically unknown to them. They have never been told that the bow has to articulate the music." Szigeti letting others speak for him, the inveterate interpreter. But am I an interpreter too or just a memorizer? I'm full of rage, fact. I'm brilliant and worthless,

fact

fact. Unorthodox bowings heighten expression, fact. Artur Schnabel: "Safety last!" Szigeti, goddamned prevenant: "The urbane, smooth style (of young violinists) . . . has no doubt been conditioned and molded by respect, not to say fear (just say it!), of the microphone and the monitor in the recording booth." And so today: everyone's engineered, parted out, mechanical, like wearing lubed prophylactics on each finger of your left hand. O, but Music itself is so rigorously strange that there's no such thing as strange music. And music, infinite, universe-tuning music, has failed me. Why am I even holding this ridiculous log? For the fire, this piece of junk jewelry? RETURN TO PROP DEPT. Not anymore, too late. I, now, could just about afford this, and then I'd be broke, chapter eleven, all I own. And then I could just wander around with it, stand on roofs, fiddling away for the insomniacs. Yes, I'm a terrorist, you're my hostages, but I'm the only victim. Tell me this isn't inspirational for you, no? A deepening experience? A character-builder? Some advice for the departed violinists? Become failed violinists if you aren't already, failed violinists better known as violists. There's absolution in failure, strange success, metaphysical redemption, just ask Judas. And as violists they should also give it up. Stop even listening to the stuff. Grow earlids. *Détaché* yourselves, *non legato*. Who likes it anyway? Who finds this dreck enjoyable? No one — it's all pretension, a put-on. And I play better and better the less and less I have to lose. I don't even own a plot. I had three, sold them, settlement, divorces, and what's involved in obtaining a divorce from one's self, ask my lawyer out there, tell him to begin billing, in his box, season tickets, a subscription for those

who

who don't own mitts, because if you did, I'd pitch myself on out, let a shvartze run home with me so he can remember to his grandkids, all medicine-breathed in *a punta d'arco / á la pointe / an der Spitze* voice — opposite being at the *frog (al tallone / au talon / am Frosch)*, me, on a Lilly which was my mother's name, the piano teacher of my uncle, did I ever tell you that I was conceived at a music lesson? my father's younger brother mother's pupil, then Father came to pick Uncle Dan (then Danny) up and then the quick wedding, no spread to speak of and no, no, no music, with a disgraced rabbi officiating like he wasn't getting paid, and not that music wasn't allowed then, it just wasn't allowed (as per the same rabbi's decree) in instances of a quite obviously knocked-up bride, knocked-up with me that is, my parent's only son, their only child three months on and showing like nine already at the musicless wedding . . .

THE CHILDREN'S CHORUS

Is the son coming up, which one? — everyone have cafeteria coffee on hand? I'll bring the salt, yes, and Dina laughs, beautiful girl, shayna punim and all babble to you. What can I do for you, Dina dear? and if you weren't my daughter I'd be seeing you after the show in my suite, but that's not couth, no. I'd pluck you pizzicato, those nipples, I shouldn't. Are you still dating that schmucky lawyer, what do you see in him? — certainly not me. And you talk in such high natural harmonics, I forgot. No, Daddy will not come down and hold you, though he wants to. Why not a policeman for you, a fine husband? — there're many here today. No, not appropriate — I have work

to

to do, what do you think you, not you, pay me for, pay for me, but I've never paid for a woman, not that I haven't had the opportunity but that I hadn't wanted to add to the motherload of surety whores must place in the patronage of artists. And anyway, all the whores I've ever met have always looked like my daughters, and I imagined this even before I ever had a daughter, and I ended up having all too many — in the 50s, in the 60s, in the 70s, even in the 80s, my 80s. In 70s fashions they looked sumptuous, in 80s fashions equally sumptuous, just updated for the 90s fashions in which and when they looked as sumptuous as ever, on into the new millennium. In which my girls are positively stunning — how I'd tell them that and they never listened, understood, took it to heart: it was always too fat (it had to be), too anorexic, bulimia-teeth, nose too long, ears too droopy, but what do they expect from their genes? and why do they believe it? when all they have to do is to look in the goddamn mirror, the best mirror: me, their father, who loves them, who loves you despite being unable to, you hear me? who sings through all the pained long-distance silences, person-to-person from all the great capitals of the world: Antwerp, Buenos Aires, Cleveland, Dresden, Elmira, Frankfurt, Gettysburg where I played the foreign anthem at some anonymous TV ceremony, Hamburg, Ithaca, Jupiter, Kansas City, Leningrad no more, Montreal, New York, New York — capital of the ego, the jutting Big Idea of a truly, and unfortunately, diseased brain floating, barely, in the Atlantic. Here where I take taxis everywhere I go because I'm a patron of the arts. Here in my stifling hotel penthouse where the dog on the record's label merely humps the dead gramophone like it's a dead-end job it

needs

needs to finance, bankroll, any higher aspirations, which are, of course, needless to say, unattainable.

Daughter Nina's higher aspiration: concert violinist like her daddy, then, when she couldn't cut it, concert violist, then just any old violist in any old orchestra. Now: a professional Jewish housewife.

Daughter Dina's higher aspiration: to be the first female president of the U.S. Now: a mother to twins and occasional freelance journalist on music.

Daughter Lena's higher aspiration (yes, I listen to you): Harvard and then a (female) rabbi. Now: attended Bennington (Harvard passed on her) and a wife, mother of three, plays the organ at the church she converted to.

Son Amiel's higher aspiration: poet, world-worshipped. Now: basement poet, bard of the hot-water-heater.

Son Michael's higher aspiration: painter, world-loved but not, he would add, world-understood. Now: dead of cancer, liver.

But it's important to understand that I had no aspirations, ever, higher or otherwise, I just was, always, already forehead-formed, Athena with a putz, perfect already.

Whereas Schneidermann's sexual life in this great nation can be reduced to the phrase: *mental masturbation*, but there was, possibly, what is known as a bag lady who had allowed him to penetrate her through a hole in her bag, but, again but, that possibly might serve as an example of his always eccentric, idio-syncratic to at times just not very funny sense of humor. I do remember, though, one time and as per Picasso I was treating him at a finer French restaurant, Chez Something or Other, and

how

how, after we'd ordered and ate and the check came, to me who was overtimes better dressed (Schneidermann pre-rumpled in a house jacket), and Schneidermann tried to foist off a musical sketch fountainpenned (my pen) on a napkin to pay for our bill, he thought overtimes to pay for it, but all they did, the management's manager, was add the price of the napkin onto our bill because it was a linen napkin and walking afterwards, Schneidermann never apologizing, whereas I was always apologizing, always, Schneidermann instead of apologizing told me that he'd received a letter, a communiqué, written on a pillowcase of and from an elderly admirer (all our admirers are elderly or just seem like it), a pillowcase written on in one account: lipstick, or blood, or burnt matchstick, giving an address in far uptown New York verging on the Bronx and how Schneidermann he went, nothing else to do, he walked, he always walked whereas I always take cabs everywhere in this town because I'm a patron of the arts, and he walked higher and higher and higher, losing two shoes and he would've lost three if he'd had that many feet, and maybe he read the address wrong, probably, definitely unless it was a joke, but who's desperate enough to play a joke on a ninety-year-old Hungarian-Jewish Schneidermann? And the city was deserted, up this high where no one can breathe, near the unicorns frolicking at the Cloisters, past the mint newsstands and bundled papers, running now past the abandoned blocks, running on beer-bottle shards, malt-liquor turds, ash, motor oil, thick vomit, oblivious to bare bloodied feet, not slowing, dripping a flower-juice trail, I come to the address specified but it's an abandoned building. I'm holding flowers, feeling especially gay in the old meaning,

ready

ready for love and women, always ready for love and
women because, at heart, I am a staunch admirer of Western
Humanism, but the building looks condemned, a ruin, all the
windows boarded-up, to crumbling around the spaces, except
one, on the top floor, in the center, a window filled by an
American flag hung there vertical, stars atop, stripes striping
down, an old flag then of 48 states (don't ask me why or how I
counted), and then, standing outside debating, Socraticizing
myself as to whether or not I should try, enter, if then then, a
baby comes flying out the American flag window, thrown out to
fall six stories, maybe seven, and, thankfully or thanklessly
depending, landing on some high hedges as the American flag
flaps back into coverage and I stand there, walk back backwards
two blocks, three, impossible to find a cab in the neighborhood,
in the whole upper demographic, but I find a limo idling and I
tap on the glass until the shvartze rolls down the window and I
offer him 100 bucks to bring me downtown and leave the bou-
quet of lilies of the valley in the limo's backseat, dripping no
more. And all the walking reminding me of shoes, of lost shoes,
but which Schneidermann referred to, with no little irony, as
life. Understand that Schneidermann had two shoes, one pair of
shoes, sizes too large for him, sizes too wide, and when he
walked they'd invariably fall off, one or the other or both, and
he wouldn't notice until he got home and took off his shoes at
the door (the Old World and Asian custom), and then he'd
notice and wouldn't leave the house (the apartment I have to
sort out) again until I'd returned his shoe, or shoes, back to
him. Because it was my lot to find his shoe or shoes (he never
bought a new pair, couldn't afford them and he got this pair

from

from the worst-dressed army in the world: the Salvation). And I'd hunt the circuit, the few blocks around his apartment building for a shoe or shoes, his shoe or shoes, and then return it or them to him, pacing the six blocks up and six blocks down and around his, Schneidermann's, ill-health confined him to, except if he was headed to the movies — Spielberg's movies especially gave him strength, energy, intestinal fortitude — and these shoes were often scattered, or shoe, against a curb from when he didn't raise his feet, his leg or legs, high enough, and the curb would pry his shoe or shoes off, or two different curbs, and there his shoe or shoes would be, lying in the street, often soaked, wedged in a sewer grating (never stolen, never irretrievably lost), and their owner would go shuffling around in his home, his house, his apartment, shoeless, unshod, like a Judean prophet or a wild Appaloosa on the plains of Jeroboam, like a man named Jesus the authorities took in for just being honest, Jewish, Roman, all the huge-German-A Authorities, and then they nailed him up to the North Pole, and set fire to him at high noon on the Fourth of July, by the Gregorian Calendar of course. And so now let us praise the firefighters, police and emergency medical personnel who have all seen fit to assemble here tonight, to coax me down off this perch . . . this frog smoking on his perch . . . I salute you gentlemen, and I hear women out there, am I right? Don't be afraid, but don't be too hasty. Allow me my allotted time, until the union quits or gets time and a half which is impossible even after Einstein — allow me my seventy plus years of age. And, yes, I've micturated on my trousers again, drip, drop of water torture — lucky I listen to the old nonadage: *semper ubi sub ubi* — dripping down to

pool

pool in my handmade alligator leather shoes, squash squish no, that's not my age, it's my fear of, *jeté.* But you might wonder to yourselves if I'd written something, if I've prepared what's known of as a prepared statement instead of just emptying my head all over Schneidermann's posterity. Well, I have, here it is, in one of these pockets somewhere, on Grand stationary, one of these — no, this one's not slit yet . . . so I didn't pocket the handkerchief as much as just steal it, pretend to blow my schnozz out into it, expel my sinus-stoffe . . . but it's not a new tux (I'm not that permissive), it's old concert dress, hospital black — or here, in one of these interior breast pockets, the slit one, here it is all crimpled and crumpled up, spilled early scotch on it and late coffee:

I leave my entire estate to the man in Row AA, seat 100.

That's the last seat in the last row of the hall, cheapest ticket — sorry standing room people, only I need someone respectable as an executor, someone who feels passionate about something. And that's as far as I got. But do I really mean to commit suicide tonight? Answers, later, to follow, at the reception, again: save your stubs. Quick! someone, some clown run in from the wings and shpritz me with some seltzer water. Because they really soak you in here. Come on — you're not picking up on it? You're supposed to yell: *You're all wet!* that's one half of the house, and the other half's supposed to shout, after the first half's finished: *You're all washed up!* Get it? Come on and heckle! — now that the Law's in on it. Get some overripe Joisey fresh tomatoes in here from the bodega on the corner (I'm tired),

and

and some jujubeans again I'm asking and how many times? I'm tired. At sea. Like I was in steerage practicing fingerings on a length of rigging rope while Schneidermann . . . with whom I'd been touring and then the War — me living in London, him dying in Poland — and then the visas came through, after I pulled some strings (G, D, A and E to be precise), and into New York, New York under the sign of Lazarus' metal flame. And yes, I'm all washed up, wet. Yes, I'm a Marinor, entering, wet, just trying to survive the soliloquy, pacing and fretting my how long's it been? since I've been here, onstage, apace, pacing and not fretting on a violin, my skull in my hand, kindled thoughts — my father's skull, Schneidermann's, everyone's all fractured and then krazee-glued together, again. Contemplating this bust of Homer, who antiquity deliberately represented to us as being blind. Another lie! To emphasize poetry's music over its written down form. You want to talk epic? let's talk epic, but we haven't the time. Because I'm busting a contemplation of Homer. Or an interpretation of Homer, because all I am, ever was and will never be again, is an interpreter, a Romantic when Romance demands and a Classicist when it pays. Standing alone, that's what Orpheus was, the only Romantic among the Classicists, the man who stood up there and had the nerve to shatter the old things, the hubris to think, screw you Ecclesiastes! there is something new under your sun, Apollo's. (The mistake of every soloist, initial motif of the Cadenza of History I'm only a germ of . . .) Because Orpheus made art a religion and religion an art, and in doing so he did the greatest thing anyone could ever hope to do and that is to give the world something to die for. Because Tchaik was a suicide too, the

pederast

– 185 –

pederast, and Mozart was short, and then there's short Stravinsky who wanted to be Mozart but failed as I'm failing Schneidermann now by not playing his unplayable concerto to the press gathered here, to the amazing, terrible and fanatic accuracy of ever-improving recording equipment — hear a woman fart underwater in another hemisphere, in the Budapest baths — and the difficulty of achieving a consistent violin sound night from goddamned night after goddamned night, transfigured, have together (recording, sound) encouraged a mode of teaching which emphasizes an all-day every-day vibrato, intense, dazzling lefty fingerwork, and uniform, even, powerful bowing. But who cares about this anyway? Too many goddamned privileges to understand how our dead had earned them for us. As the world taught me and I heard people, in Romania, around Sighet, old Satmer stomping grounds, play better than that, faster too. But this style wins laurels and makes green money greener with envy for other money already made, wins competitions and so here, in this town, damned be the dead Ivan Galamian and Dorothy DeLay the bitch (poetic justice too long delayed) — teachers of too many of today's young virtuosos, goddamned Asians with no explosion, no real immolation of the soul, and laugh at me! but I never had a stand partner, never played ensemble, not even quartet to sit-in at a daughter's wedding, and not because I don't like people (I do and I don't), or the literature (Beethoven! Bartók! Shostakovich! Even some young who think they're Europeans, who don't exist anymore) but who cares for others if I can't even care for myself? I have only myself to worry about, and who has life enough for anyone else? But what do you say Alana,

give

give me a second go at it? — you look great, and with Dina and all. No Jeremy, leave her be. She's a mother of my children, and sad to say sort of my mother too — you do the math, which has nothing to do with music: that's just the intellectuals and the Classicists trying to out-eunuch each other, as if Maria could care less, as if you could care less, even though you want to get your money's worth, even though you need to witness my failure, need to destroy me by remaining silent there in your sprung seats, in these halls where I'm reborn, these church and synagogue auditoriums and college, university amphitheaters, later master classing in their lecture halls — all these amalgamations of glassed-in existences ingathering from the aesthetic diaspora as part of an annual subscription series, and me cranking out the same hits every time, over and over and over again, windup musicbox, mechanical bird. Because I'm a memory machine, Schneidermann's performing retarded masturbating monkey, a symbol with the cymbals, insipid and hallelujah so! Because only one thing happened in my life: the violin. My early years listening to the town klezmers, then up late in Berlin and Paris listening to older violinists on 78s and, at first, admittedly, this can be a bit unpleasant, shocking. Because we've grown fond or expectant of that thick throb, the wall of sound between ear and violin, us and music. But once that's swept away, the violinist seems naked, vulnerable, weak and maybe, yes, effete, impotent, ineffectual, light in the shoes, less of a man. But it's the still small voice! Me? Who masturbated on trains. Music. On planes. In my long life. In limousines. The same twelve tones over and over again, related to whom, Schönberg, your two beloved Nazis? Nothing after,

no

no children and grandchildren even. On boats. Music was me. More precisely the violin was me. I should be listened to as a great lieder singer — I'll lied you to water, and there you'll drink until I let you drown, and can I get the glass I asked for, or maybe not, almost three or four hours ago? I've stopped time, at 4 AM already . . . hours past the whiching hour, when usually I'd be passed out on the floor of my hotel room, heating full on, while watching a pornographic movie on mute, reading Wagner and eating lactose intolerant, lo-fat ice cream to lose this weight, this stomach vibrato I've got to get rid of. O realize how much we've lost, you've lost! How the violin's range has been reduced, but who cares? How Schneidermann's been forgotten and who cares? How Schneidermann once took a shit in a piano, onto the soundboard, a bonewhiter at some party, a duchess, feet on the keys, tapping out Beethoven's *Ninth*, pants around his ankles, the melody, the fraternal muzak, the first sell-out, his turds vibrating sympathetically some strings, and everyone shocked except the servants. But this is not what an artist does (if he does, he's a fake) — this is what art itself does, is. No, this is an apology, not for him, but for me. Because I've never done anything (except this, and this is a pity, pitiful), never done anything real, huge, exploding, aaaaaaahhh . . .

Yes, an applause-beg. I've read my stage directions.

Abraham storms stage right, undertone.

They're so detailed, aren't they? — they become more and more detailed with each passing line, just as the wrinkles become more pronounced on this punim of mine I hope is seared into your eyeballs for all time, the face of destiny, yes, but more accurately the face of one who has failed destiny,

preserved

preserved forever in a moment exposed, unposed, not like the portraiture of my youth when we'd take three days to get ready and the photographer would have to get the imported palms angled just so and then one last time for my mother, all mother, to rush in and spit my face back into composure, the faintest Mona Lisa smile held not in the mind or the mind's eye but in time, for the exposure to spend itself and earn its keep on the mantle. The money's in the band to the back, hat hung on the rack in my dressing room — save the redeeming ticket left in your other head — along with a will for my manager's eyes only, stipulating that guy whatever your name is and I don't want to know in Row AA, Seat 100 and some vodka and slivovitz there on the *vanity*, appropriate word, going back to my roots and forsaking the scotch and whiskey, and three encrusted monogrammed handkerchiefs containing what could conceivably be three children or more because my seed's still strong, have any doubts? and I should tie my tongue in a bowtie now, before . . . which makes me look like a monkey anyway, and so I am that I am, which I've also read and heard read to me in the original and could repeat to you if you cared enough to listen. Why does everything require your pledge-driven generous support? Never forget the free tote bag. Why can't someone or thing just succeed honestly in this world, on his or her or its own merit?

Like me — but I can't play this thing! I want to die, not slow Yiddish death, 2nd Ave., but fast, immediate, must rid myself . . .

. . . die, die, die, die, die and then . . .

. . . I've smashed this into, this violin — and this should be

a

a Yiddish or at least a Yinglish word — into *smithereens* . . .

A waste? Its worth is priceless, I don't own it. Stick of a bow snapped over my knee. Why not? Gasp. Vomit. Not mine to waste.

Because I've turned Asian women into observant Jews, I'm sick. Jappish they speak. *Mushi-mushi, is here Sarah* and the like. Because I've made mistakes, left out notes, which ones? slowed down metronome markings, freely interpreted difficult passages, and so what? They are what made me. Splinters at my feet. I am them and they are me, I'm a mistake then and what're you going to do about it? I'm a fraud and that pisses you off because you paid for this, and own my albums, and now you have to radically revise your cocktail/dinnertable opinions. Because I've had my difficult passage, and now I want to die. Because I've smashed my violin which isn't mine. Dead. So approach! Because I am worthless, and the whole world has mislaid its mental apparatus, lost the instructions and the markings, and no one knows what's good and what's bad anymore, and what would it matter anyway if they did? and last week Schneidermann killed himself maybe or maybe not by allowing himself to go insane and disappear one day from his welfare hole at nearly a hundred-years, leaving behind only shit, history (his first, last and only estate) and his *Concerto*, which I haven't explained yet, will never be properly finished, again . . . no movement in the future, understand? And so that's your cue, officers, your entrance. Time for you to approach the royal presence — it's in the to-be-evened score — you badges, bluemen, courtiers from the empire most foreign, empire of decorum, empire of politesse, empire of fat and happiness, and

applause

applause on the palm, light like we're at tennis . . . Schönberg and Stravinsky playing on a court set in the world's largest martini-glass, in Beverly Hills, while Uptown's Schneidermann ate his ears . . . when this involves death, a Romantic death where nothing's going to resolve in the end — you goddamned Classicists who don't even know what Classicism is, your comedy and tragedy masks without ears, frayed veins in fluted marble . . . don't obtain permission, get clearance, don't! — come, rush in, where everyone fears to tread, you who are left and haven't been here before because the State doesn't pay you adequate salaries. I propose raises all around, and all the precincts get a night at the opera every week with presentation of badge and bullets and gun, but what good would that do you utter Americans? Instead, home asleep you vide soaped-up operas, lathered in human fat, then the hang for the next installment — me on the morning news, tomorrow . . . and so allow me a stationed break in the way of sorrows and advertisement for some Thomas Taylor, whom the Americans (Emerson most notable among them) read and not the Europeans, because no one even now at history's end is able to resolve preference and empirical value:

> *Thy fleep perpetual burfts the vivid folds,*
> *By which the foul, attracting body holds:*

I'm so tired that I can't even differentiate between the two. I'm so tired that I can't even kill myself. I'm so afraid that I can't even kill myself. Too afraid as all poets are, as all artists are, as all prophets are, all afraid of not being a martyr. And so

someone

someone betray me besides myself! someone martyr me! and you're coming! yes! finally! — come, don't walk, run! to embrace a lost brother who stole the age's birthright, and you'll bear the gifts of silence. I mean you all have guns, so use them! a big boom, a kettledrum, the firetruck New York, New York sound and the anvil of Mahler . . . but, wait, no, we haven't even gotten to Mahler yet, so wait, hold-up, Schneidermann, yes, in any revival he was eclipsed, but Alma . . . Now, no gag, allow a man his honor, yes, by the shoulders, and dignified . . . Alright, three steps back, and bow to the silence. Because what else is there to respect except those things that are not? Because there are some things left unsaid, unevoked, and they are art. Because what can we realistically expect of ourselves? Being as nothing from nothing, hanging by our fingertips from the lowest rung of the angel's ladder, and we've now all lost that past footing the bill. And so we scream! Everyone, all together now! And Rilke too! I apologize — where's my memory?

> Sei immer tot in Eurydike —, singender steige,
> preisender steige . . . moment . . . zurück in den reinen Bezug . . .

. . . and wait, no . . .

Okay, so lead me out.

I'll never remember it all, but I will lead the processional, up the red carpet for my coronation . . .

. . . a crown of stars, and not back through the wings, no, under the balconies and down the center aisle, out the lobby and front door into winter, Christmas soon with the tree going up amid . . .

. . . new

. . . new doors, aren't they? Yes, I expected them waiting for me . . .

Everyone enjoy the reception — you are all working overtimes forgiven.

And, yes, is it snowing out?

And soon . . .

Soon . . . soon . . .

O the lit air.

ACKNOWLEDGMENTS

Much of the material on Orpheus found in "Schneidermann" is from, or has been influenced by, W.K.C. Guthrie's excellent *Orpheus and Greek Religion: A Study of the Orphic Movement*, in the Princeton University Press, Mythos edition of 1993.

Another exhausted source of mine for Orphica was *The Hymns of Orpheus Translated from the Original Greek with a Preliminary Dissertation on The Life and Theology of Orpheus to which is added the Essay of Plotinus Concerning the Beautiful* by Thomas Taylor (1758-1835), which I own in a "facsimile reprint of the original English edition of 1792" (Los Angeles: Philosophical Research Society, Inc., 1981).

The *Hymns'* most evident typographic design, one widely used in English literature of the 18th century, in which the first word of a next page is given hanging below the margin at the end of the page previous — less an aesthetic element then than a reading aid — I lifted for use in "Schneidermann" because of its felicitous similarities to musical cues as given on individual instrumental parts. These cues are given so that a musician, whose hands might soon be occupied with playing, does not have to waste few moments — moments better spent in physical and mental preparation for an entrance — on turning pages.

A few lines were lifted from Salomon Reinach's Introduction to his *Orpheus: A History of Religions*, first translated into English, from the

French in 1930, and now published by the Kessinger Publishing Company, Kila, Montana, year unspecified.

Paul Celan's poem beginning "Die Posaunenstelle," quoted in "Schneidermann," is from his collection *Zeitgehöft* (Frankfurt am Main: Suhrkamp Verlag, 1976).

All other uses, such as my quoting of William W. Hallo's translation of the second edition, 1930, of Franz Rosenzweig's *The Star of Redemption* (University of Notre Dame Press, 1985) in "A Redemption," should, I hope, be evident.

Thanks to the editors of the following publications where earlier versions of these stories have appeared: *Est*, *Fiction Warehouse*, the *Forward*, *The Modern Word*, and *Prague Literary Review*.

Joshua Cohen was born in 1980 in New Jersey. Having spent time in New York and Israel, he lived in Prague for a number of years working as a journalist, essayist, and editor for many publications, including the *Prague Pill*, *Prague Literary Review*, *Czech Business Weekly*, and the *Forward*. His short fiction has appeared in many journals and anthologies, such as *Glimmer Train* and *The New Book of Masks* (forthcoming 2006). A recipient of first prize in *The Modern Word*'s 2003 Short Story Contest and short-listed for the Koret Foundation's prestigious 2005 Young Writer on Jewish Themes Award, Cohen is currently Arts Editor of *New York Press*.

TITLE: The Quorum

AUTHOR: Joshua Cohen

COVER IMAGE: Markéta Hofmeisterová

AUTHOR PHOTO: Ahron Weiner

TEXT: Perpetua

DESIGN: Bóbo Dál

PRINTING & BINDING: Tiskárny Havlíčkův Brod, Czech Republic

PUBLISHER: Twisted Spoon Press: www.twistedspoon.com

TRADE DISTRIBUTOR: SCB Distributors: 1-800-729-6423
info@scbdistributors.com / www.scbdistributors.com

This is a first edition published in 2005